The Return of the Earl

Joan Wolf

Untreed
Reads

The Return of the Earl
By Joan Wolf

Copyright 2021 by Joan Wolf
Cover Copyright 2021 by Ginny Glass and Untreed Reads Publishing
Cover Design by Ginny Glass

ISBN-13: 978-1-95360-158-2

Published by Untreed Reads, LLC
506 Kansas Street, San Francisco, CA 94107
www.untreedreads.com

Also available in ebook.
Printed in the United States of America.

Publisher's Note

Note on Class

Social class in Regency England was rigid and most of the time unbreachable. As class plays an important part in the plot of this novel, I would briefly like to clarify a few points.

British aristocracy was a closed society. It consisted of a limited number of families who socialized with each other and married each other. Duke is the highest non-royal title; then comes in order: Earl, Viscount and Baron. These are the Lords of England who sit in the upper house of Parliament. They and their offspring were the people one would see when they gathered at social occasions during the season and at house parties in the summer and autumn.

Next in importance was the landed gentry. They were not regarded as noble. Baronets did not sit in the House of Lords. They might be called "Sir" and their wives referred to as "Lady," but to the aristocracy the members of the gentry were "not one of us."

In regard to this novel—it would be highly unusual for an earl like Lord Chiltern to marry a baronet's widow like Laura, even though she carries the title of "Lady Aston."

Chapter One

It was a lovely summer day and I had taken my daughter out to play on the front lawn. She was three years old, and the energy packed into that small body never ceased to astonish me. She might wear me out, but I loved every moment that I spent with her. It was when she was napping, or asleep for the night, that all of my troubles came rushing back.

I was losing my house and I didn't know where Rosie and I were going to live next. My husband had died recently, and the new baronet wanted to move in. If Rosie had been a boy I wouldn't have been in this horrendous situation. A boy would have inherited the title and the house and all would have been well. Instead, Tom killed himself after gambling away a large sum of money, leaving Rosie and me both penniless and homeless. He had not been a good choice of husband.

My father wanted us to come live with him but I didn't want to do that. I adore my father. He is the vicar of a parish near Hastings, and he had been both my father and my teacher during all the years I was growing up. He had been wonderful to me when Tom died. Our local vicar had refused to bury him in consecrated ground because he was a suicide and Papa had stepped in and quietly buried him in his own churchyard. He had also given me the money to pay off the shopkeepers in town to whom Tom owed money. Papa badly wanted Rosie and me to come and live with him, but I couldn't.

Five years ago my father had remarried. His new wife, who had been sweet as candy before the wedding, turned into a poisonous snake once she had his ring on her finger. One of us clearly had to go, and I was only the daughter. There was but one solution to this impasse and I took it. I married Sir Thomas Aston, a tall, blond young man who was a baronet and who originally seemed perfectly amiable. Unfortunately he had turned out to be a reckless gambler who ended up killing himself because he couldn't pay his debts.

So here I was at twenty-three, a widow with a child, with no home and no money. Every night I lay awake, trying to find an answer to my desperate situation. I had the education to become a governess, but I also had a daughter to support. And Papa had Violet.

I loved my father but I was angry with him. I didn't want to be, but I was. He had been enough for me; why hadn't I been enough for him? Why had he married that woman? If it wasn't for her I would still be living happily at home with none of this burden on my shoulders. Papa wanted me to come home, but I could not subject my little daughter to the poison that woman would certainly pour into her ears.

What could I do? Where could we go? The new baronet had threatened to involve his solicitor if I didn't move out within the next two weeks. I was desperate. What could I do to earn money for Rosie and me?

*

I was throwing a ball back and forth to Rosie a few days after I had received the new baronet's ultimatum, when a very elegant carriage turned off the road and started to come up my drive. Fear closed my throat. It must be the new baronet with his solicitor come to evict me.

"Mama!" Rosie called. "You didn't catch it!"

I ignored the ball and reached out a hand to her, "Come here, darling. Let's see who might be in this carriage."

Rosie came running and slipped her small hand into mine. "Is it that bad man who made you cry?"

Unfortunately she had been present at my last meeting with the new baronet.

The carriage stopped and the coachman jumped down to open the door. He set the carriage steps and a woman appeared in the door, her expensively gloved hands holding her skirt so she could descend safely. I recognized her immediately. It was my godmother.

"Aunt Rose!"

Then she was crossing the lawn to me holding out her arms. "Laura, darling, how lovely to see you again!"

I felt her arms close around me and inhaled the scent she always wore. Some of the tension in my stomach relaxed. Aunt Rose was here.

She loosened her arms and I stepped away. "I am so happy to see you, Aunt Rose!"

"I have been in Paris so I didn't hear about Sir Thomas' death. Really, Laura, ever since that horrible Napoleon was forced to abdicate, I believe there are more English people in Paris than French. It is quite festive but the earl wanted to get home. It wasn't until I spoke to your father that I learned about your husband's death."

"Come inside," I said. "You are just the person I want to see. I am being evicted from my house and I need some advice about what to do next."

I felt Rosie tugging at my skirt and bent down to pick her up. She's a sturdy child—she's built like her father—and it wouldn't be long before she was too heavy for me to lift.

"This is your goddaughter, Rosie," I said.

"Hello my little namesake." Aunt Rose smiled at Rosie. "How you have grown! I have brought a little gift for you."

Rosie's brown eyes widened. "You have?"

"Yes, I have. Let us go into the house and I will show you."

I put my daughter down and straightened up. "You will stay the night?"

"If it's not too inconvenient."

"You could never be inconvenient, Aunt Rose."

We walked together to the front door, which was opened by the only servant I had left, Becky Shaw, a local girl who helped me with a little bit of everything.

Aston Hall is a pleasant, comfortable house. It boasts six bedrooms, a drawing room, a morning room, a dining room and a small library. It is not unlike the house I grew up in, and when I came here as a young bride I had pictured Tom and I filling it with children. Tom would be a wonderful father and a careful steward of his property. I would involve myself in the life of the church and the village, as I had done when I lived with my father.

That dream had died quickly.

I took my godmother into the drawing room. Becky brought in Aunt Rose's baggage and my godmother produced Rosie's gift, a beautiful French doll. Rosie's eyes almost engulfed her face when Aunt Rose put it in her little hands.

After Rosie had made her proper thank you, I sent her upstairs with Becky and asked Aunt Rose if she would like tea. She accepted and I said apologetically that it wouldn't take but a minute for me to put a tray together.

Aunt Rose stared. "Surely you are not preparing the tea yourself? Have you no servant to do it?"

"I have no money, Aunt Rose. I had to let all the staff but Becky go. Papa gave me the money to pay their back wages. Tom hadn't paid them in months."

I left my stunned looking godmother sitting on the sofa and went downstairs to the kitchen. I had baked scones in the morning so there was something to put out for tea, but I wondered what I could possibly give my aristocratic godmother for dinner.

I made the tea, put the scones on the prettiest plate I had, then arranged them all on a silver tray. I went back into the drawing room with a smile pasted on my face. I was going to have to beg Aunt Rose to help me and I hated having to do that.

We took our first sip of tea and Aunt Rose said, "Your father told me you were coming to live with him. Is that wise? Can you bear to live with that awful woman he married?"

I stared into my half-empty teacup. "I do not want to go back to Papa, Aunt Rose, but this house and property are entailed and

Tom's cousin, the new baronet, is panting to move in. I've wracked my brains about what to do because I *don't* want to go back to Papa. Not because of Papa, of course. You know how much I love my father. But his wife is a vicious woman, and I don't want Rosie subjected to her hurtful comments."

Aunt Rose shook her head. "I never understood why you married Thomas Aston. You had a half-dozen fine young men who wanted to marry you; why did you pick *Aston*?"

"I rejected those proposals because I didn't want to leave Papa. He's the kindest sweetest man in the world and I didn't want to leave him alone. Then that woman came along. She saw how good-looking and kind Papa was. She saw how nice Papa's house was. And somehow she convinced him to marry her.

"The servants resented her becoming the mistress and came to me for everything. She hated me and said unspeakably nasty things when Papa wasn't around. The atmosphere in the house was poisonous, Aunt Rose. Papa was caught between the two of us and he was miserable. One of us had to go, and she was the wife.

"I picked Tom because all of my former suitors had already married someone else. I met Tom when he was visiting a friend in the neighborhood and they came one night to a dance at our local assembly rooms. He began to court me."

I sighed in bleak remembrance. "He was young and handsome and a baronet. Papa spoke to him about his finances and Tom convinced him that I would have both position and financial security. It seemed at the time he was a gift from heaven. I married him."

"Do you have any sherry in the house?" Aunt Rose asked.

I was surprised by the question but thankful I could oblige her. "There's a bottle in the library. I'll go get it."

When I returned with the bottle and some glasses, Aunt Rose was standing by one of the windows that looked out on the side garden. She heard me come in and turned around. "Your flowers are lovely."

"Thank you. May I pour you a glass of sherry?"

We returned to the sofa and sipped our wine. Then Aunt Rose put her glass on the table in front of us and turned to me. "I believe I may have a solution for you that is more acceptable than returning to your father's rectory." I sat with my hands clasped so tightly in my lap that my knuckles were white. "Before I came here I paid a visit to my nephew Robert, the new Earl of Chiltern."

Aunt Rose was the daughter of a previous Earl of Chiltern and I said quickly, "Oh Aunt Rose. I read in the Morning Post about the carriage accident. What a tragedy. I am so sorry. Both the earl and his wife were killed. How is the new earl managing?" The earldom had gone to the second eldest son, who was in the army.

"Not well," Aunt Rose said. "Robert never expected to inherit. He never wished to inherit. He always wanted to go into the army."

"The earl didn't leave any children?"

"He did. Two little girls. Margaret is ten and Elizabeth is six. Unfortunately, Robert was next in line." She sighed. "He has been in the army since he was eighteen years old. He's twenty-six now and has hardly ever been home. The earldom is a huge and unexpected responsibility and he's a bit overwhelmed."

"I can imagine," I murmured, thinking it was hard to feel too much sympathy for a man who had just become one of the richest men in the country. I finished my sherry, put my glass down and said bluntly, "What does this have to do with me, Aunt Rose?"

"When I was visiting Robert at Chiltern Hall he told me that Lord Castlereagh had asked him to join Wellington in representing England at the Congress of Vienna. I must say, Robert is an excellent choice. He was with Wellington in Portugal and all through Spain and France. And now he bears the title Earl of Chiltern, which is one of the oldest titles in England. Wellington himself told Castlereagh that he wanted Robert in Vienna and Robert feels he has to go. The Congress is convening in September and he needs to leave immediately."

Aunt Rose picked up my hand and held it in a warm clasp. "Chiltern Hall is in a state of confusion and Robert cannot leave the children with only the servants to look after them. The girls have a nursemaid and a governess and the hall has a housekeeper and butler as well as the usual staff. What Robert needs is a chatelaine, a woman of the upper class to supervise the servants and make certain the children are being looked after properly." Aunt Rose squeezed my tense hand. "This is a perfect answer to your present situation, Laura. You are a lady. One sees that the moment one meets you. The servants will respect you and Rosie will have two other little girls to play with."

I thought about what Aunt Rose was saying. It might be only a temporary solution but it was better than going home to Papa. And I had no other options. "How long would his lordship be away at this conference?" I asked.

"Several months I imagine."

I was thinking hard. "Is there a salary attached to this position?"

Aunt Rose looked surprised, but then she smiled and patted my hand again. "I am certain there could be. Robert has inherited great wealth."

I summoned up a smile and said, "Under those circumstances, I will take the position. Thank you, Aunt Rose, for thinking of me."

Chapter Two

A week later I received a letter from Aunt Rose. She wrote that the earl had already left for Vienna and in two days' time she was sending her carriage to bring Rosie and me to Chiltern Hall.

It had been a struggle to hide from my daughter how worried I was about this move. Yes, the position had been a gift from heaven; but I had no experience in running a great house like Chiltern Hall. I had grown up in a rectory and my married abode had been the house of a gentleman. Both houses had been roomy and comfortable and we had employed a few servants. Chiltern Hall was one of the Great Houses of England! An unbridgeable chasm existed between my way of life and the way of life at Chiltern. How on earth would I, Laura Aston, fit into such a place, let alone manage it?

I flew around, packing our meager belongings and trying to reassure Rosie that she would be happy at Chiltern, that there would be two other little girls to play with her and wouldn't that be fun. I held her hand tightly as Aunt Rose's carriage pulled out of our driveway. I did not look back; I was finished with Aston Manor.

Aunt Rose's carriage was wonderfully comfortable and our journey took only a few hours. Rosie was sleeping with her head in my lap when we turned into a long, tree-lined drive. I awakened her so I could put her hat back on, and I smoothed out the wrinkles of my traveling dress. I was sitting straight up against the squabs, not looking out the window, when the coach stopped. Our door was opened, steps were set so we could alight, and for the first time in my life I laid eyes on Chiltern Hall.

I had known it would be magnificent. I had known it would be big. But I had not been prepared for this. It was as if one had stumbled upon an Italian Renaissance palace in the midst of the mellow English countryside. A great dome dominated the building, which stretched out in graceful elegance over what looked like countless acres. To the west of the house was an avenue of cedars, which I would learn led to the stables and the hothouses. To the east was a glorious deer park studded with fine old oaks and graceful ponds. A marble fountain was the focal point on the enormous front lawn.

We stepped onto the graveled path and Rosie slid her hand into mine. "Is this where we're going to live, Mama?" she whispered.

"Yes, darling, we are," I said with false cheerfulness.

Rosie's little fingers squeezed my hand, and I knew exactly how she felt.

*

The massive front door opened, Aunt Rose stepped outside the door and held out her arms in welcome. Three white-wigged footmen followed and went to the carriage to bring in our paltry baggage. After hugs all around, Aunt Rose ushered us into the house.

The entry hall was enormous. The floor was black and white marble tile, and the walls were hung with paintings I knew must have cost a fortune. Two people were standing inside and Aunt Rose first introduced the butler, Mason, a tall, upright man who looked to be in his fifties. He bestowed a stiff smile upon us, bowed and said, "My lady." The housekeeper, Mrs. Lewis, a well-padded woman in her forties, curtsied and said, "My lady."

Rosie's grip on my hand kept getting tighter and tighter and I said to Aunt Rose, "I think Rosie would like to meet Lady Margaret and Lady Elizabeth. Might we go up to the nursery?"

"We have something to discuss first, Laura," Aunt Rose said. Then, to the butler, "Will you have tea brought to the Blue Salon, Mason? I am sure Lady Aston and Miss Rose must be hungry and thirsty after their journey."

Rosie's big brown eyes looked up at me. I said, "Might we have lemonade as well, Mason?"

"Of course, my lady." The butler bowed and disappeared, as did the housekeeper. We followed Aunt Rose into a very large room papered in blue silk and lined with more priceless paintings. We sat on one of the elegant sofas and Rosie pressed tightly against me.

After she had established herself Aunt Rose said in a grave voice, "We have a small problem in regard to the children, Laura. Their governess left yesterday for a position in London. It was very unexpected, and I think her behavior in this matter is atrocious. She gave us no notice at all. Really, I am very put out."

I was startled and made murmurs of agreement about the perfidy of the governess. As Aunt Rose continued ripping the character of the departed governess to pieces, I had a happy thought. Governesses made money.

Once the earl returned to Chiltern Hall my position here would be finished. If I became the governess to his nieces, however, I might be able to remain. Even if he didn't wish to retain me, I thought that if I could say I had been governess to the Earl of Chiltern's nieces I might be able to find another position that would include Rosie.

Aunt Rose, however, was not amenable to my offer to act as governess to the girls. Instead she informed me she had great plans to find me another husband once my mourning period was officially over.

This generous offer fell on fallow ground. I had no plans to marry again. Once had been more than enough for me. I did not confide this information to Aunt Rose, however. I didn't want to say or do anything that might disturb the happy accord that prevailed between us. We drank tea and talked and talked and I finally managed to convince her that I would like the governess position because it would allow me to be close to Rosie. I also convinced her that the pay I had been awarded for acting as chatelaine should be increased if I were to take on the position of governess. I'm afraid she found my conversation about money rather crass, but when you don't have any money you can't afford to be high minded.

Aunt Rose remained at Chiltern for a week, helping me to "settle in." She was very helpful in that she modeled for me the sort of supervision the servants would expect, but to be honest I wasn't sorry to see her leave. I wanted to spend more time in the nursery than I had been able to while she was in residence.

*

Rosie and I settled into life at Chiltern Hall with surprising ease. The earl's nieces had not liked their previous governess, but they seemed to like me. Margaret, the elder, was bright, and teaching her was a pleasure. Elizabeth was a little more difficult. She had a strong personality and I had to walk a fine line between reprimanding and praising her. The most important thing to me, however, was that both girls liked Rosie and treated her as a little sister.

There was one person who lived at Chiltern that I had not yet met—the earl's steward. When I first arrived at the hall he had been on a visit to some of the earl's other properties and he did not return until I had been in residence for some weeks.

Mason, the butler, had assured me that Mr. Kingston was a gentleman, and that he (Mason) hoped I would not mind taking my dinner with him. I had replied truthfully that I would appreciate the company. I had been uncomfortable dining by myself, with Mason and a footman waiting on me as if I were a queen. I would have preferred to eat with the children in the nursery, but the earl's very correct butler had been horrified by that suggestion.

When Mr. Kingston walked into the drawing room a few minutes before dinner on the day of his return I almost made a fool of myself. I had been expecting an ordinary middle-aged, middle-class man. Mark Kingston's chiseled features could have been copied from a statue of Apollo. He stood several inches over six feet, his well-cut hair looked like spun gold and his eyes were a deep dark blue. He was stunning.

I mumbled a greeting and tried not to stare. He must have been accustomed to such a reaction because he took my hand and said in a normal voice that he was pleased to make my acquaintance. I recovered my composure and we went into the dining room together.

I had been eating in the small dining room that Mason called the breakfast room. There were two other dining rooms in the house. One was large and elegant and was used when the entire family was gathered. The other was mammoth and breathtaking. Several paintings by Titian decorated the walls in that chamber. The breakfast room had only one large Van Dyke.

Mason had changed my place from the head of the table to the middle, with Mr. Kingston sitting across from me. This made it easy for us to converse and, somewhat to my surprise, I found this paragon of male beauty comfortable to talk to.

After we had finished Mrs. Minton's roast and excellent apple pie, we moved our conversation into the gold salon. I used only three rooms on the ground floor of this enormous house: the gold salon, the morning room and the library. I liked the gold salon because it had a comfortable sofa, the morning room because it was pretty and informal, and the library because it had books.

Mr. Kingston and I arranged ourselves, me on the comfortable silk-covered sofa and Mr. Kingston in a highbacked chair at right angles to me. We chatted over tea and discovered that we were both the children of clergymen. Mark's (we had got on a first name basis rather quickly) father had a parish in Derbyshire and Mark was the sixth son. "I never quite knew what I was going to do with my future," he told me.

"How did you come to get this position?" I asked.

"I went to school with Robert Daubeny, the earl's second son, and I gave his name as a reference. We weren't in the same class—I was two years older—but he must have told his father good things about me because I got the post."

Mark's presence was a blessing to me. I no longer had to endure long lonely meals, and from our upbringing we had many things in common. I never felt lonely when Mark was at home.

Chapter Three

The *Morning Post* was delivered to the house every day, which allowed Mark and I to follow the progress of the Congress of Vienna. For months all we learned was that the representatives of the various nations couldn't seem to agree about anything. On the other hand, the Congress appeared to be a huge success socially. The newspaper informed us in some detail about the balls and masquerades and other dissipations that went on till all hours of the morning. I pictured the absent earl twirling around dance floors with beautiful princesses and duchesses in his arms. It would be nice if he liked Vienna so much that he decided to stay there.

I was happier here at Chiltern than I had been since I left my father's house. My duties were very similar to those I had shouldered at home, but the scale of things at Chiltern was much grander. I worked hard to learn the names of the huge number of indoor servants and also the names of all the grooms in the stable, as well as the names of the gardeners. It took a small army to run Chiltern Hall and I couldn't even begin to imagine how much money it must cost to keep it going.

Part of me wanted to relax and enjoy this very pleasant situation, but another part kept reminding me that it was only temporary. I was earning money now—good money. Aunt Rose had authorized a very generous salary for my services as chatelaine and governess. It was the answer to my prayers, and I had to focus on the future, not luxuriate in the ephemeral present, enjoyable though it was.

By January it appeared that the delegates were close to an agreement on the final disposition of the countries once conquered and ruled by Napoleon. Mark and I read that Lord Castlereagh had departed from Vienna, leaving the Duke of Wellington in charge of completing the Congress' Final Document. Since the Earl of Chiltern was one of Wellington's aides, I was confident that he would be remaining in Vienna as well. My hope was it would take a long time to complete this Final Document. The more money I could accumulate, the brighter the future would look for Rosie and me.

Then came the event that shook the world. On March 1, 1815, Napoleon Bonaparte escaped from his prison on the island of Elba and landed on French soil.

"He's going to raise his old army," Mark said soberly as we sat in the morning room having tea.

I felt a shiver run down my back. Would we really be going back to war with France?

In the following weeks, as Napoleon made his way across France, the soldiers of the army that had once conquered most of Europe flocked to his flag. On March 20 a triumphant Napoleon entered Paris and received a rousing welcome from the populace. The Emperor was back.

While Napoleon gathered his army, an allied army was mustering in Belgium. Mark and I read in the newspaper that the Duke of Wellington had been appointed as the army's Commander in Chief and he had departed from Vienna to join his troops.

A battle between the two greatest commanders of their day, perhaps of all time, was inevitable.

We prayed in church for our army, and we prayed for the Earl of Chiltern, whom we had learned for certain was at Wellington's side.

*

On June 5 I was in the nursery with the children when Charles, our youngest footman, informed me that Lady Baldock had arrived. I told the girls to stay with Nana, their old nurse, and went downstairs to greet her.

Mason had put Aunt Rose in the largest reception room in the house except for the Great Hall. This magnificent room was filled with priceless paintings, vases, statues and furniture. It belonged in a palace and was rarely used. I briefly wondered why Mason had chosen it. Perhaps he had thought the magnitude of the times deserved such a setting.

When I came into the room Aunt Rose advanced toward me, arms extended. I hugged her back. "Come and sit down," I said when she finally let me go. "Have you news of the earl?"

"I received a letter yesterday. It was written just before he left Vienna with the duke. They are both in Brussels by now, waiting to go into battle with that *Monster*."

I let out a heavy sigh.

"Have you any brandy, my dear?"

"Of course." I had been about to order tea but changed the order to a bottle of brandy and two glasses.

We sat side by side on an uncomfortable brocade sofa, holding hands and saying little until Charles came in with a tray. Aunt Rose filled her glass and mine. She finished hers in a few swallows. I took a few sips of mine and watched her.

"You're afraid for the earl," I said when she had put her glass down for the second time.

"I am terrified for him." She poured some more brandy. "I keep telling myself that he will be fine. He will survive. God wouldn't be cruel enough to take Robert too. This family has suffered enough."

I didn't think God had much to do with who lived or died on a battlefield. Human beings had the power over that, not God. But I kept my opinion to myself.

"Oh Laura!" My name came out as a sort of wail. "If Robert dies, the next in line for the title is Horrible Harold!"

I don't know what I had expected to hear but it certainly wasn't this. "Horrible Harold?" I repeated in bewilderment.

"He is the eldest of my brother's nephews and a disgrace to his name. He must *never, never* inherit the title! It would be the ruination of us all!"

I said, "The earl has managed to survive battles in Portugal, Spain and France, Aunt Rose. He must know how to take care of himself."

"He was wounded twice," she returned. "What if his luck has run out? What will become of the family? What will become of the children?"

I did my best to calm her but I wasn't very successful. She stayed for dinner and paid a visit to the nursery to see the children. By the time she had finished exhorting them to pray for their uncle's safety in this terrible upcoming battle, she had managed to terrify Margaret and worry Elizabeth.

Aunt Rose always slept in the room that had been hers before her marriage, and by the time I said goodnight to her and went upstairs to my own bed she had me almost as frightened as she was.

My bed was in the nursery and I lay awake a long time, my mind in an uproar. I had to make plans for Rosie and me. If the earl died, and this Horrible Harold came to live at Chiltern, I did not want to be here.

Papa only lived two hours away and he had been to see us several times. He wanted me to come home. Violet had changed, he told me earnestly. She was much more tolerant than she had been when first she moved into the rectory.

Privately I thought that she was more "tolerant" because I wasn't there. If I returned, the hostility would return as well. I had a plan in mind, but it would require some time before I could realize it. I might have to go back to Papa, but it would only be for a short time.

My busy mind wouldn't let me go to sleep, and at about two o'clock I heard a tap at my door. As I called out "come in," I devoutly hoped it wasn't Aunt Rose.

The door opened slowly and a familiar head peeked in. It was Margaret.

The nursery at Chiltern was large, spreading across many rooms. I was living in the governess' quarters, which was a spacious apartment including a bedroom and sitting room. A large playroom separated my quarters from the children's rooms. The playroom was a treasure trove of books and toys, and there was an area with a stove where I could fix hot chocolate and tea. The children's bedrooms were on the other side of the playroom. Nana's room was on that corridor as well and so was the nursery maid's. The children had adults sleeping nearby.

When I saw Margaret's tearful face I held out my arms and she ran to my bed and scrambled in, burrowing into me like a little animal. I held her, stroking her hair and making soothing noises until the crying tapered off.

My heart bled for her. In less than a year this child had lost both her parents, and now her uncle, her guardian, might be killed as well.

I had always hoped the earl would stay away from Chiltern for a long time, but now, as I held this fragile child in my arms, I realized how selfish I had been. His nieces needed him, needed the security of his presence in their lives.

Margaret lifted her tear-stained face. "What if Uncle Robert is killed, Lady Laura? Who will take care of us then? Will we still live here? If we can't live here where will we go?"

I had no answers for her. All I could say was that there would always be someone to take care of her, but we must keep praying that Uncle Robert would come home safely.

She eventually fell asleep, but I lay awake for the rest of the night, Margaret's cry sounding over and over in my mind. *If we can't live here where will we go?*

*

On Sunday, June 8, the battle for a continent was fought in Belgium at a place called Waterloo. Napoleon's re-unified Army of France stood against the Allied Army comprised of British, Belgian, Dutch and German soldiers, all of them under the command of the Duke of Wellington. Wellington was also supported by the Prussian Army under the command of Field Marshal von Blucher.

At the end of a day-long battle the Allies were victorious. Napoleon was defeated. According to the newspaper, the casualty count on both sides was enormous. Mark and I counted the days as we waited to hear if the Earl of Chiltern had been among the survivors.

Aunt Rose brought us the news. The earl had survived and would be coming home shortly. Jubilation reigned at Chiltern and in the local village. Our prayers had been answered.

My feelings were conflicted. My happy life here at Chiltern was bound to change with the return of the earl. And…I didn't want to leave Chiltern. First, I was saving a substantial amount of money. And second, I was enjoying my new position. I had made friends at church, and I helped with teaching the Bible Studies Program for Children. Margaret and Elizabeth were part of this program and they liked it. I had grown very fond of the girls and would hate to leave them. I had also grown fond of the staff—particularly Mason, who hid a big heart under all that outer stiffness.

Once again my future loomed uncertainly before me. I knew nothing about the earl, but I told myself that he had to be better than Horrible Harold.

Chapter Four

It was a lovely July evening a few weeks after Waterloo, and we had not yet heard from the earl. I was sitting in the morning room after dinner reading a book I had taken from the library shelves. It was an English translation of the plays of Sophocles and I was entranced. My papa was a classical scholar, but he had been very careful about the books he allowed me to read. When I saw the English translation on the shelves, I immediately pulled it out. What could Papa have been hiding from me?

I had read *Oedipus Rex* and was immersed in *Antigone* when Mason came into the room. I looked up and he said, "Lady Aston, his lordship has just arrived. I have put him in the gold salon."

My heart began to thud. I put my book down and said, "I will come."

My heartbeat didn't slow as we walked down the hallway. *The earl is here. The earl is here. What am I going to do with him? He's here— and Mark's away. I'm on my own. Dear God, help me to get this right."*

I walked into the salon and saw a man standing in front of one of the tall windows looking out at the deer park. He must have sensed my presence because he turned to face me. I said, "Good evening, your lordship. Welcome home."

He left the window and came toward me. My first swift look showed a man of medium height and black hair who held himself like a soldier. When he reached me I looked up into light gray eyes framed by long black lashes.

He said, "I'm sorry not to have given you some notice, but I finished up at the Horse Guards this morning and thought I might as well come down. I didn't fancy spending another day in London."

His speaking voice was crisp and clear. A good voice for giving orders.

I said, "We are very glad to see you, my lord. Your nieces and the entire staff have been praying for your safety."

He looked surprised but didn't respond.

I said, "Have you eaten, my lord? I'm sure cook has something left over from dinner."

"I'm fine." The gray eyes, which appeared very light against his tanned face, looked at me as if taking my measure. "You are the woman my aunt hired to look after the children and the staff. I'm sorry, but I don't remember your name."

I could feel the color rushing to my face. "I am Lady Aston, my lord, and I am indeed the person your aunt hired."

The very word *hired* made me wince. But I couldn't accuse him of insulting me. I was receiving a salary. I had insisted on receiving a salary. I was in fact the hired help.

I had no idea what to do with him. He was wearing riding clothes so I said, "Would you like to change your clothing, my lord?"

"What I would like very much, Lady Aston, is to retire to my bedroom. I'm rather tired."

I said, "Of course. Since we did not know you were coming I'm afraid the earl's bedroom suite has not been made up. If you wouldn't mind waiting, Mason can bring you some brandy."

He sighed. "The earl's bedroom suite...I suppose I shall have to sleep there." He shrugged his shoulders as if trying to rid them of a burden. "Just have a maid throw some sheets on the bed. I'll take the brandy and a glass up with me and wait until she's finished."

I could see the weariness on his face. I rang for Mason, who appeared immediately. "His lordship is fatigued, Mason. Will you have a bottle of brandy and a glass brought to the earl's bedroom and have one of the maids put fresh sheets on the bed. His lordship is tired and would like to retire."

"Of course, my lady." He looked at the earl and smiled faintly. "You do look a bit worn, my lord."

The earl flashed a return smile. "I am that, Mason. It's been a long day. But it's good to see you."

"It is *very good* to see you, my lord. Do you still like peppermint candies?"

At that the earl grinned and years fell away from his face. "I do," he answered.

"I'll see if I can find some. You go on upstairs Mr. Rob...*my lord!*" He looked horrified at his mistake.

The earl waved his hand dismissively. "It doesn't matter, Mason. Just don't forget about the brandy."

"I won't, my lord." Mason had recovered his composure. "Will your valet be coming?"

"He should be here tomorrow with my clothes, but I can see to myself for tonight." He looked at me and said courteously, "Good night, Lady Aston."

I curtsied. "Good night, my lord.

*

I did not sleep well that night. It had finally happened. The earl had returned and my uncertain future yawned before me like the jaws of a great black cavern. I did not want to leave Chiltern. Rosie was happy here. Also, I didn't have quite enough money saved to buy a house and open a school for young ladies.

That was the future I had planned for myself and my child. Both my mother and Aunt Rose had gone to a boarding school for young ladies. It was where they had met. Why couldn't I be the owner of such a school? With enough tuition flowing in to keep us, I would finally have the independence I craved.

I had to convince the earl to let me stay on as governess. I needed to stay on as governess. I knew I had begun to think about Chiltern as my home and I knew that was a dangerous way to feel. But I couldn't help it. Rosie was not the only one who was happy here. If I could stay for a few more months...or perhaps even a year...I would have the money I needed to set myself up as the owner of a school for young ladies.

I finally fell asleep, and when I awoke I decided to follow my usual routine and go down to the stables. The Head Groom, Walsh, an Irishman, had become a friend. He said I was a gifted rider and that he was fortunate to have me to help keep the horses exercised.

I had cherished that compliment. I was proud of my riding. While I was growing up Papa had always kept a horse for me, and I had taken Magic with me when I married. Unfortunately, he had colicked shortly after Rosie was born and had to be put down. The only horse left to me in the Aston stable had been an old gelding I used to pull the pony cart into the village. In contrast, the Chiltern stables were filled with beautiful horses, and I treasured my morning ride.

I had thought I would be safe, that the earl would sleep late, but as I approached the stable I saw a black-haired man dressed in riding clothes talking to Walsh. It was the earl.

I had been surprised last night by that black hair and slim body. For some reason I had expected him to be big and blond. Both his nieces were blond and so was Aunt Rose. I hesitated, not knowing what to do, but Walsh saw me and waved me over. I bit my lip in indecision, then slowly approached the two men.

Walsh beamed at me and said to the earl, "Lady Aston is a very pretty rider, Mr. Robert. The reason the horses are going so nicely is largely due to her."

Before the earl could respond, Walsh clapped his hand to his mouth. "I called you 'Mr. Robert!' I'm sorry, my lord. Habit is a hard thing to break. It won't happen again."

The earl's smile radiated warmth and charm. "There are very few people left in this world to call me Robert. I would like very much for you to be one of them."

The Irishman flushed with pleasure. I wasn't surprised. That smile was devastating. "Sure, and you know I love you like a son," Walsh said.

"I missed you more than I missed my family," the earl returned, and I could see he meant those words. "I am very happy to see you again, Walsh." He put a reassuring hand on the Head Groom's shoulder and Walsh turned even pinker.

The earl then turned to me. "How are you this morning, Lady Aston? Are you going to join me for a ride?" His voice was quietly courteous.

Like Walsh I flushed. "I am well, my lord. I have enjoyed riding your horses very much, but you will want to take your first ride at home without a stranger for a companion. I shall return to the house and hope to see you later."

The earl looked relieved, but then Walsh said, "You must ride, Lady Aston! I'm after having two horses saddled. Cachet for you and Romeo for his lordship." He turned to the earl. "You won't mind having such lovely company, Mr. Robert, now will you?"

"Of course not," the earl said in the same quietly courteous voice.

Walsh had put the both of us in a pretty position. It was clear to me that the earl didn't want my company, but if I refused again it would seem churlish, and if he refused it would seem discourteous.

At this point two grooms came out of the stable leading Cachet and Romeo. Romeo was looking at Cachet with interest but she was ignoring him. I looked at Walsh, raised my eyebrows and said, "An interesting choice." Cachet was a saucy chestnut mare barely fifteen hands high and Romeo was a dark bay seventeen-hand gelding.

I said to the earl, "Romeo is aptly named, my lord. He doesn't always remember he's a gelding."

He laughed.

He went up to Romeo, put his foot in the stirrup and swung up onto the huge horse as if he were as small as Cachet. I mounted the mare and together we exited the stable yard and headed for the woods.

Romeo tried to get closer to Cachet as we walked along and was corrected gently but firmly. Cachet carried herself as if Romeo didn't exist. I wasn't worried about her. I knew all her tricks and she knew I knew them. She would be fine.

In fact, both horses were fine, and we had a very pleasant gallop along the lake. When the horses had come back to a walk and we were heading back to the woodland path, the earl looked down at me and said, "Can you explain to me what precisely is your position at Chiltern Hall, Lady Aston? My aunt was not very clear about it. Can you enlighten me?"

I glanced at him. His eyes were focused ahead and I regarded his chiseled profile thoughtfully. I patted Cachet's shoulder to keep her focused on me and answered, "Aunt Rose asked me to live here during your absence because she didn't think the children and the house should be left alone without supervision for such a long period of time. That is why she asked me to live at Chiltern and act as chatelaine until you returned. I had just lost my husband and I was free...."

I let my voice peter out. I hated to have to admit how pitiful my situation really was.

He said, "I'm sorry about your husband."

I stared between Cachet's pointed ears, gathered my courage and said very fast, "Aston Manor was entailed so I could not remain there and, since my husband had gambled away all our money, I had no place to go. Your nieces' governess had left for another position before I arrived, so I have been acting as their governess as well. I have become very fond of them and would be happy to stay on as governess, if that would be acceptable to you."

I could feel him looking at me, but I kept my eyes focused between Cachet's ears. My stomach was in a knot and I didn't want him to see how much I needed this position.

He said in a calm, level voice, "I will not be making any changes in the household at present, Lady Aston. You are welcome to continue with your present duties."

My body sagged with relief. "Thank you, my lord," I said and my voice quivered.

Mercifully, he changed the subject. "You call my aunt 'Aunt Rose,' but she isn't really your aunt, is she?"

I straightened my back. "She is my godmother. My mother and Aunt Rose were at the same boarding school and they became close friends. I have always thought of her as part of my family. She's my daughter's godmother as well."

He looked down at me from the height of Romeo's back. "She's my godmother too." He added with amusement, "She must be quite a professional by now."

I laughed. We rode for a little in silence, then I said, "The children have been looking forward to meeting you."

There was a little silence. Then he said ruefully, "It is a very long time since I have been around children, Lady Aston. I hope I don't disappoint them."

There was a crackling sound in the woods next to the trail and suddenly five deer burst out of the trees and raced across the path in front of us. Cachet whinnied and reared. When she came down she backed up and bucked. When I had calmed her, we resumed our place at Romeo's side. She walked on like a saint. I said to the earl, "She loves a drama."

He laughed and ten years magically dropped away from his face.

I said, "Margaret and Elizabeth need you, my lord. They need the security of knowing someone is responsible for them, is taking care of them." I told him about Margaret's visit to my bedroom before the battle and ended by saying, "This child has lost both her parents. From what I gather they were often away from home, but Margaret always knew that her world was secure. Then there was a carriage accident and everything changed."

He looked very sober. "I see. I will do my best to assure her—and Elizabeth too—that their lives will go on as they always have. It is fortunate that you will be able to stay on, Lady Aston. I'm sure your presence will help to reassure them that nothing about their lives will change."

"Thank you, my lord," I said.

"Shall we trot for a bit?"

"Certainly," I replied, and we sent our horses forward again.

Chapter Five

I didn't see the earl for the remainder of the day. When I asked Mason his whereabouts the butler told me he had gone into the village to visit Chiltern's solicitor. "He told me he would be back for dinner, my lady, and Mrs. Minton has prepared his lordship's favorite dinner, roast beef with Yorkshire pudding. She always made it for him when he came back from school as a lad." His face wore a reminiscent smile. "We were all that fond of Mr. Robert."

I next asked, "Does the earl expect me to join him for dinner?"

Mason looked astonished. "Certainly, he does, my lady. We can't have him eating alone!"

"I suppose that would not be good for him."

Mason favored me with a smile. "Allow me to say that I am glad you are here, my lady. I do not think it would be good for his lordship to be alone just now."

I smiled at Mason and we parted.

*

I usually brought the children downstairs after they had finished their tea. After all, Chiltern Hall was their home. They should see more of it than just the nursery.

This day was like all the others. I had tea, Margaret and Elizabeth had lemonade and Rosie had milk. We usually sat around the tea table in the morning room and talked about whatever subjects the girls might be interested in at the moment. Today we were discussing the problem of the poor. Margaret at age 10 and Elizabeth at age 6 were old enough to come to church with me on Sundays, and the sermon the previous Sunday had been about our duty as Christians to help the poor. Elizabeth had asked me where the poor lived because she never saw any.

I was speaking about poverty and where it was found and how it could be helped when the door opened and the earl came in. I stopped talking and he waved his hand, "Please, Lady Aston, don't let me interrupt you. I have only come to meet the girls."

"Come and join us," I invited him. He came and sat on the sofa next to me and I presented his nieces to him. I ended by introducing Rosie, "And this is my daughter, Rosie, who is sharing the nursery with your nieces."

"I am very pleased to meet you Rosie," he said gravely. "I am pleased to meet you all. Now that I have become responsible for your welfare it is important that we get to know each other."

"Are you going to take care of us?" Elizabeth asked.

"I am going to take very good care of you. I am sorry about your Mama and Papa dying, but I am here now and I will make certain that nothing in your lives changes."

He was looking at Margaret as he spoke. Margaret sat up a little straighter and said, "We are happy to have you at Chiltern Hall, Uncle Robert."

"I am happy to be here," he replied.

"I'm happy too, Uncle Robert." Elizabeth did not want to be left out.

"I'm happy too, Uncle Robert!" Rosie joined in the welcome.

"Oh dear," I said to the earl. "I thought I had explained to her that you were not *her* uncle. I'm sorry, my lord."

Elizabeth said loudly, "I told her too, Lady Laura. I told her Uncle Robert was *our* uncle, not hers."

Rosie began to cry.

The earl said, "I would very much like to be your uncle too, Rosie. Would you like to be my niece?"

The tears disappeared and Rosie beamed. "Yes!!"

Elizabeth started to object and the earl said mildly, "My relationship with Rosie has nothing to do with you, Elizabeth."

He locked eyes with her; she looked down at her hands and muttered, "I suppose it's all right. if you say so."

"I do say so."

I said, brightly, "We have been discussing the problem of poverty, my lord. It was the subject of the Vicar's sermon this

Sunday. Elizabeth wanted to know where the poor lived because she never saw any."

He looked interested. "I saw many poor people when I was in Portugal and Spain, and England has many poor people too. I'm certain there are poor people here in Sussex. Perhaps we could try to do something to help them."

Margaret's solemn face brightened. "I would like that, Uncle Robert."

We discussed this interesting topic until one of the maids appeared to take the children upstairs for their dinner. After they had left, the earl turned to me and said, "You appear to be doing a very good job with them, Lady Aston."

His voice was quiet, almost uninflected, but I felt a rush of pleasure at his acknowledgement. "Thank you, my lord," I said.

He rose to his feet. "I hope I will see you at dinner?"

"Yes, my lord. And I have it on good authority that Mrs. Minton is preparing roast beef and Yorkshire pudding for you."

His eyebrows lifted. "How nice of her to remember. The rest of my family liked to eat French food, but I have always had a taste for plain old English roast beef."

"With Yorkshire pudding," I said.

He nodded. "With Yorkshire pudding."

I watched as he went to the door. He walked fluidly, balanced on the balls of his feet. He was not like I had pictured him at all.

*

I next saw the earl in the gold salon as we both awaited the summons for dinner. His valet, a Scotsman named MacAlister, had arrived and he appeared faultlessly dressed in evening clothes: a perfectly fitted black coat, a white shirt with an expertly tied cravat, and fawn pantaloons. I had not expected him to be so fashionable, but then I remembered he had been in Vienna for the past year. Mark and I had read about the extravagant social life in Austria's capital during the time of the Congress.

31

He gave me a grave smile and came into the room.

"You made a good impression on your nieces," I said with a smile. "They could talk of nothing else."

"I hope I made them comfortable. Such young children should not have to worry about their futures."

I nodded agreement and brought out the little speech I had prepared. "I also want to thank you for being so kind to Rosie. The girls treat her as if she was a little sister and it's hard for her to remember that she isn't of their class."

"Elizabeth needs to learn to keep her opinions to herself," he said pleasantly.

I defended my charge. "She is only six, my lord."

"I doubt that Margaret would have said such a thing at her age."

"Margaret is a very kind little girl," I said. "Elizabeth has a strong personality and I am endeavoring to teach her to think more of others."

"Like the poor?"

I smiled. "Like the poor."

Mason appeared in the doorway to announce dinner. The earl offered me his arm. Under the fine material his forearm was hard as iron. Mark had always offered me his arm but I had never felt as nervous as I did right now, walking into the dining room with the earl.

Two places had been laid, one at the head of the table and one at the foot. I shot Mason a surprised look. The lady of the house should sit at the foot. Mark and I always sat in the middle of the table facing each other.

The earl went to his place and as I started toward my new position, he turned to Mason and said, "If you wouldn't mind, Mason, I would appreciate your putting Lady Aston at my right hand. I'd rather not have to raise my voice every time I address her."

"Certainly, my lord." Mason looked at one of the footmen who was standing with him and the footman hurried to bring my plate and cutlery to the appropriate space. When my new place had been properly laid, the footman escorted me to my seat.

"Thank you, Tim," I said as he pushed in my chair.

"My lady." He was one of the older footmen and I liked him a great deal.

The earl noticed him for the first time. "Tim! How nice to see you are still here at Chiltern. How are you doing?"

Tim colored with pleasure. "I'm well, your lordship. It's that glad we are to have you safely home."

"Thank you. We shall have to play a game of chess one of these days."

Tim's face got redder. "I would like that Mr....Your Lordship!"

The earl said to me, "When I was five years old I asked Tim to teach me to play chess. We became fierce rivals over the years."

"Ah, it didn't take you long to figure out how to beat me, my lord. It was that embarrassing, being checked so fast by a ten-year-old lad."

Our wine glasses had been filled and the earl picked his up and turned to me. "Have they been giving you the good wine, Lady Aston, or fobbing you off with the mistakes?"

Mason began to say something but quickly muffled himself. The earl didn't look at him but a smile tugged at the corners of his mouth.

"Whatever I have been given to drink, it was always excellent, my lord," I said.

I glanced at Mason; he looked gratified.

The earl's lips twitched again.

We both took a sip of our wine and he began to eat the soup. I took a spoonful of my own but found I wasn't hungry. I was too aware of the man sitting next to me to feel comfortable enough to eat.

I looked at him out of the side of my eyes as he ate with appetite. His hair was black as ink, as were his eyebrows and eyelashes. He had defined cheekbones, a narrow, arched nose and a perfectly sculpted mouth. And there were those extraordinary light gray eyes. He was a very good-looking man.

We conversed pleasantly as dinner was served. I asked him how his visit to the solicitor had gone. "My head is still spinning." His tone was humorous but the look in his eyes was serious. "I wasn't brought up to be the earl. I always knew I was destined for the cavalry. The transition is rather intimidating."

I thought that he didn't look like a man easily intimidated. "Chiltern is rather large," I said.

Tim came to take away our soup dishes and Mason placed a large roast beef in front of the Earl. "Mrs. Minton thought you wouldn't want to waste your appetite on a fish dish this evening, my lord," Mason said. "She made quite a large roast beef for you."

The Earl looked down at the huge roast beef in front of him, looked up at Mason again and grinned. "I could have fed my whole regiment on this," he said.

That grin made him look like a boy.

"It won't go to waste, my lord. I can promise you that."

"I'll make certain to leave enough for the servants," the earl retorted.

We ate the delicious food and, rather to my surprise, I found he was easy to talk to. Actually, thinking back, I was the one who did most of the talking. I told him I was the daughter of a vicar and I had also grown up in Sussex. He asked me if I liked Chiltern and I answered frankly. "It was strange at first. Here I am, the daughter of an ordinary vicar, living in the home of a great lord and acting as the lady of the house. A house I would normally only visit if I came on the days it was open to the public."

"Did you find it lonely here by yourself?"

"At first it was lonely. But I grew up knowing my responsibilities to the poor and elderly. Elizabeth may not have seen them, but there are plenty of poor and elderly in the area. And enough crippled soldiers as well, my lord. Not everyone was lucky enough to return from the war as healthy as you."

"I know all about crippled soldiers, Lady Aston." His voice was even and calm, but I could hear the bitterness underneath. "I was often the one who sent them home missing limbs—if I wasn't burying them. I will make it my business to see these men are taken care of properly. You will have to take me round to meet them."

"Thank you, my lord, I will be glad to do that."

He nodded and said, "I think I might have a little more of that Yorkshire pudding."

Chapter Six

A week later I was standing in the riding ring watching Margaret and her pony. Margaret was not a natural rider. She liked horses enough when she was on the ground and could feed them a piece of sugar, but she wasn't quite happy being on their back. Walsh told me she had taken a bad fall when she first started riding and she had not been able to put it behind her.

Walsh had recently found an elderly good-natured pony for her and Margaret loved him. She was doing well and today I had her go over a two-foot obstacle. She had screwed up her courage and Tommy, the pony, had almost stepped over it. We were finishing up when a curricle came rolling into the stable yard.

Margaret said, "Mr. Kingston's back, Lady Laura!"

"I see." I watched as a groom ran to hold the two perfectly matched chestnuts harnessed to the curricle and Mark jumped down from the high seat. He left the horses with the groom and came over to the ring.

"Riding lesson?" he asked good-naturedly.

Margaret had dismounted and came to join us with Tommy. I saw Walsh coming from the stable to take the pony. He was beaming. He must have seen her go over the tiny jump.

Mark congratulated her on her riding and she replied modestly that she was getting a little better.

Walsh came up to the curricle and ran his hand over the chestnuts' hind quarters. Mark said solemnly, "I swear on my sacred honor I walked them for the last three miles."

Walsh nodded. "Tis a warm day. We'll sponge them down and put them in their stalls with some hay."

I said, "Have you had anything to eat, Mark?"

"Not since breakfast."

"Come up to the house and I'll order tea."

"Thank you, Laura," he said in a fading voice.

Walsh took the pony and two grooms arrived to unharness the carriage horses. Margaret, Mark and I walked back to the house, with Margaret telling Mark about how she had "jumped my pony." I also informed him that the earl had returned. The humor left Mark's face at those words and we both let Margaret chatter on as we walked along in silence.

*

Mark and I had our tea undisturbed. It wasn't until dinner time, when we gathered in the gold salon to await Mason's call, that the earl made an appearance. He looked at Mark and I could see the exact second he recognized him. "Kingston!" he said. "Back at last, I see."

He walked toward Mark with his hand held out. Mark stood and grasped it firmly. He said, "It is good to see you home safe, my lord. I'm sorry I wasn't here when you arrived."

The two men dropped their hands and I regarded them with interest. The earl's slender figure looked almost boyish in comparison to Mark's superior height and breadth, but there was something about that slender figure that more than counter-balanced Mark's greater size.

We went into dinner and I saw that a place had been laid for Mark on the left side of the earl. I wondered if Mason had decided this or if he had consulted the earl.

The soup was served and we ate. As we waited for the next course the earl said to Mark, "Lady Aston has told me you were visiting some of Chiltern's properties. How did you find them?"

"I was not completely pleased with the situation in Derby, my lord. We have rented it to a couple who have three daughters. They are gentry but aspiring to something higher for their girls. I have a feeling they are a little short of the blunt. They've missed the rent three times since they moved in. Spending too much money to impress the neighbors, I think."

"Too bad," the earl said. "Perhaps we should have investigated their finances before we rented to them."

That *we*, of course, meant Mark.

Mark regarded his employer with an expressionless face. "I had them investigated, but apparently I did not receive the correct information. Do you wish me to evict them, my lord?"

"No." The earl's voice was firm. "Not until I have a chance to look over the books myself."

Mark did not look happy with this comment. The earl said, "Perhaps the daughters will marry rich men and all will be well."

I should have let this comment pass, but I didn't. I said, "It is not very pleasant for a woman to know that the future of her family rests upon her marrying someone she scarcely knows for his money."

Both men turned to look at me. I had not expected my voice to sound so bitter. I ate some of my fish and ignored them.

"Sometimes men are in the same position, Laura," Mark said. "Many men have been forced to marry heiresses to keep their estates from being sold."

"It's not the same thing," I said.

"No, I suppose it is not the same," said the earl slowly.

I glanced at him and found him looking at me. His gray eyes were grave. I gave him a fleeting smile.

Mark said stiffly, "Most of your estates are up to date with their payments, my lord."

"I don't mean to criticize you, Kingston. I saw my solicitor yesterday and was staggered by the size of Chiltern's holdings. I grew up as a younger son and so was not privy to the financial details of the earldom."

Mark said, "Your inheritance is vast, my lord. As Earl of Chiltern you own estates in Derbyshire, Yorkshire. Lancashire, Lincolnshire, Cumberland, Sussex, Middlesex and Kent. You also own an estate in Scotland and a castle in Ireland."

I could feel my eyes growing larger with every name Mark brought forward.

The earl said, "So my solicitor informed me. Apparently I am also the patron of various clerical livings for which I am responsible to make appointments."

He sounded rather grim.

I said, "Many people may be depending upon you, my lord, but this is an opportunity for you to help them."

The two men looked at me and I realized how preachy, vicar's-daughterlike I had sounded. I flushed. "I'm sorry…" I began.

The earl smiled. "Never be sorry for saying something kind, Lady Aston."

That man should have his smiles strictly rationed, I thought with annoyance. They were far too potent to be allowed free rein.

The earl excused himself after dinner. He had some matters to attend to and would be in the library if anyone needed him. Mark and I retired to the gold salon where I queried him shamelessly. "You knew him when you were at school. What was he like?"

"He always stood out. Whether it was in scholarship or in sports, he stood out. The masters always chose him whenever a leadership position opened. Frankly, I never understood how he did it. He never pushed himself forward. He wasn't a big talker. But the boys always chose him to be captain of every team he played on. And it wasn't just his social rank. He was chosen over the sons of dukes."

There was something in Mark's voice I had never heard before. Was it envy? Before I could decide, he said, "I have some good news to share with you, Laura. I enjoy my position here, but like most men I have always wanted to be my own master. And my father has just written that my Great Aunt Sophia has made me her heir."

My eyes opened wide in surprise. "Goodness," I said.

"She's always rather doted on me. She married a wealthy man and they had no children. I stayed with her sometimes when I was a boy. It was she who sent me to Eton. I suppose you might say I was the son she never had."

"Goodness," I said again. I didn't know what else I could say. I couldn't ask him how much money he expected to receive, or how old and how healthy this great aunt was.

Mark answered both questions without me having to ask them. "It's enough money for me to purchase a nice little property and have enough left to live comfortably."

I smiled. "How nice, Mark. I'm so happy for you."

He smiled back. "I'm not going anywhere just at present, Laura, but Aunt Lizzie is in her seventies."

I understood the implication but couldn't find a proper reply. "Goodness," I said for the third time.

"I'm not wishing her dead, Laura. I like it here at Chiltern." He gave me a very blue-eyed look. "I've liked it even more since you came."

I felt my cheeks flush. "I like it here as well," I said. "And it looks as if I'm going to remain as governess to the girls. The earl told me he was not interested in making any changes."

"Now *that* is good news!" Mark said emphatically.

"He didn't say anything about my position as chatelaine, however."

We were sitting side by side on the gold tapestry sofa when one of the downstairs maids came into the room bearing the tea tray. "Your tea, Lady Aston," she said.

"Thank you, Ellen." I watched as she placed it on the mahogany tea table that was in front of our sofa. "Are you feeling better?" I asked.

"Yes, my lady, thank you for calling the doctor. He gave me a drink o' something and my stomachache stopped somethin' wonderful."

I smiled at her. "Good news."

She smiled back. "Yes, it is, my lady. Is there anything else you'd be wanting?"

"No, thank you, Ellen."

When Ellen had left I poured Mark a cup of tea. While he was drinking it I said, "If I'm to continue to act as chatelaine, I should continue to be paid for that position as well as for the governess'. Do you think you could speak to the earl for me?"

For a brief moment his hand covered mine. "Of course I can, Laura."

As we finished our tea we talked easily about his trip to the north and then I went to bed.

Chapter Seven

For the rest of July life went on as usual. Mason still came to me for his orders, and I met with Mrs. Minton to plan the meals. Every week Mrs. Minton also prepared a goodly number of food packages which I distributed to those elusive "poor people" who actually lived in our parish. I did this every Tuesday. Annoyingly, Walsh wouldn't trust me to go by myself; he always insisted I take one of the grooms.

"I am perfectly capable of carrying one of those packages to each recipient," I protested every time I left. But he was adamant. "It's bad enough that you must be taking that old farm cart, my lady. There's plenty of room in the town coach for those bundles of yours. I'm not saying it's not after being a good thing yer doin', Lady Aston. But you should go in the coach."

I could not picture myself driving up to Jenny Selfly's cottage in a coach with four horses and a driver. And since the phaeton, the barouche or curricle didn't have space enough for the food packages, I took the farm wagon. I had been brought up as a vicar's daughter, not as a grand lady.

Mark had spoken to the earl about my salary, and he had doubled it! When I tried to thank him, he waved his hand in dismissal. "You carried this household for almost a year. You are still the acting mistress and, in addition to this, you teach my nieces, who seem to be very fond of you. You deserve every penny of that salary, Laura."

He had started calling me "Lady Laura" when Elizabeth protested that I wasn't "Lady Aston" I was "Lady Laura." Then, after a while, he had dropped the "lady" and just called me Laura. He had a beautifully flexible voice, and I liked the sound of my name on his lips.

I liked him. I liked him even though I knew scarcely anything about him. Often, when we were walking the horses in comfortable silence, I would wonder what lay behind that outwardly calm and perfect countenance. But I was not on such terms with him that I could ask.

*

The earl and I rode together almost every morning. He had brought home with him his surviving horse from Waterloo—a well-muscled chestnut gelding named Beau. Cachet got along with Beau better than with Romeo. Beau kept himself to himself and that was fine with her.

I also went with the earl when he rode around the estate to reintroduce himself to his tenants. The tenant farms at Chiltern were all well cared for. If a farmer needed a roof, Mark had a roof put on. If he needed a new fence, the fence went up. Mark was very popular with Chiltern's tenants, and I was curious to see how they reacted to the earl.

Everyone had happy memories of Mr. Robert. Although he had spent such a small amount of time at home, during the summer holidays from school he had apparently played ball with the sons of almost every tenant on the estate. I asked him about this as we rode home late in the afternoon. "Did your brother join in these games too?"

"George was much too high in the instep to play with the tenants' children," he said. "He was much too high in the instep to play with *me*. George was brought up to be an Earl and he never for one moment forgot his importance."

"It doesn't sound of as if you were close," I said.

"No, we weren't close."

I glanced at his profile. It gave nothing away. I said, "It also sounded as if yours was always the winning team. Did they let you win?"

For the first time he looked a little ruffled. "They wouldn't have dared." A squirrel ran across our path and Cachet decided to do a little jig. When I had made it clear that I did not appreciate such behavior, the earl said thoughtfully, "I learned a lot from those boys. They helped me become a good officer."

"What was the most important thing you learned?"

He didn't answer right away, and I was afraid I had asked too personal a question. But after we had gone a few strides in silence he said, "I learned that if you want to earn the respect of your men you must always treat them honestly and with good humor."

I thought this was a splendid answer.

We rode for a little while longer then he unexpectedly asked, "What's this I hear about you taking food to the poor?"

I was not happy with the change of subject. "Walsh told you."

"He did. He doesn't approve. He thinks you should have the food delivered by a footman."

"Do you have an opinion on this subject?"

"Yes, as a matter of fact, I do."

I had been watching the path while we spoke, and now I regarded his profile in silence. If he forbade me to deliver the food it would feel like betrayal. My hands clenched on the reins and Cachet threw her head up in protest.

He said, "I think you should take Elizabeth with you one day."

My mouth dropped open.

He added, "In fact, you should take Margaret as well."

I had braced myself to hear the worst and suddenly the sun had come out.

He was continuing, "Take them separately. Let them each see how close to them poor people are living. It's important for them to know that those who have been given much have an obligation to help those who have little."

"I will be happy to do that, my lord."

He smiled, the smile that I liked the best, the one that made him look like he was eighteen.

We rode for a few more minutes, then I said, "Perhaps one day *you* would like to accompany the girls and me on our food distribution trips."

His gray eyes were filled with amusement "Good for you, Laura. Pin me to the wall. I deserve it." We were coming to a rather steep hill as he said, "I shall be happy to accompany you to visit the poor."

He went ahead of me down the steep narrow trail and I looked at his back and shoulders and thought how lucky I was that the feared Earl of Chiltern had turned out to be Robert.

*

At dinner that evening the earl mentioned our ride around the estate and complimented Mark on the way he carried out his position. "All of the cottages look in excellent repair," he said. "The tenants had nothing but praise for you, Kingston."

"Thank you, my lord." Mark looked pleased.

"There was something else that caught my attention as we spoke to the tenants," the earl said. He put down his knife and fork and took a sip of wine.

Mark and I waited for him to go on.

"Almost all of these people have large families. I find myself wondering what the children do when they grow up. There can only be so much work on the farm, which I suppose the eldest son will inherit. He will need help, of course, which the younger ones could supply. But how many people can one farm employ?"

I was a vicar's daughter, and I was not unfamiliar with the problem. "Some of them hire themselves out to other farmers. Some of them are forced to work in the factories. Others join the army, although I doubt the army will be looking for new recruits just now."

He said grimly, "The army is dismissing thousands of men who fought in the war against Napoleon. Where are the jobs to come from for those men?"

My father had a particular interest in the problem of the poor and he had imparted his concerns to me. I said, "Many of them will return to their native villages and find that there is little work. They will be forced to work on farms as agricultural workers, where they receive a small house for which they must pay a shilling a week. They work with scythe, plow and sickle in the fields from the time when the horn booms at five o'clock in the morning until nightfall. When their houses leak or rot they are dependent upon the landlord for repairs. And unless the landlord takes care of them when they can't work anymore, they go to the workhouse to finish out their days."

As I finished I realized how passionate I had sounded, but I wasn't going to apologize.

Mark and I looked at the man who sat at the head of the table. His face was very still but his gray eyes glittered between their long black lashes. He said in a quiet voice, "That is unacceptable." He picked up his knife and fork, added, "I see I shall have to make myself known in Parliament," and he ate a slice of chicken.

It seems strange to say this, but those few simple words of his reassured me. I said, "Parliament doesn't reopen until February."

He finished chewing his chicken and looked at me. "Then I shall have time to investigate the problem."

I smiled at him.

He didn't smile back, just nodded gravely and ate another piece of chicken.

Chapter Eight

The peace and quiet of our household splintered when Aunt Rose descended upon us the first week in August. I had always been glad to see her when she visited during the period during which the earl was away. I had not been as delighted as I usually was when I received the note announcing her pending visit. Aunt Rose always had a tendency to stir the stew, and I was happy with my life the way it was.

She arrived on a pleasant late August afternoon and I greeted her affectionately. We had tea in the main drawing room; the gold salon was not good enough for Aunt Rose.

We sat, sipped our tea, ate Mrs. Minton's wonderful cake and scones, and I waited for the bomb to explode. It didn't take long. After Aunt Rose had finished her second scone, she said ominously, "I have been thinking about your future, Laura,"

"It is settled for the moment," I said quickly. "Lord Chiltern wants me to stay on as chatelain and governess to the children."

"Well you can't do that." She put her teacup down firmly and turned to face me.

"Why not?" I sounded like Elizabeth when I said this.

"Because you are unchaperoned in this house! It is not appropriate. And you cannot spend the remainder of your life as a governess."

I had no intention of telling Aunt Rose about my plan to open a school. "Why not?" I said again. "I like being a governess. I'm good at it and children like me."

"If you were a governess in any other house but this one you would not be drinking tea with me in the drawing room."

Since this was obviously true, I made the only reply I could, "I don't care about that."

"You would care once it happened. I can assure you that you wouldn't like it at all. A governess is not part of the family, she is a servant. An elevated servant, but a servant none the less. The only future for you, my love, is marriage. And I am going to help you find a husband."

"But I don't want to marry again!"

Aunt Rose looked at me as if I were a madwoman. "Nonsense. Of course you must marry again. It is the only practical answer for a widow with a child. I had to wait for your mourning year to end before I could step in, but now it's time."

I said steadily, "Marriage is not the answer for me."

She still had that look on her face. "Why ever not? What can have caused you to take this very tiresome position?"

I stared at my lap and didn't answer.

Silence fell. I could feel Aunt Rose staring at me. Finally she spoke. "Did that wretched Aston give you a bad time in bed?"

My head jerked up and I stared at her in shock.

"So that's it."

I could feel my face burning and I looked away.

She reached over and took my hand in hers. She patted it gently. "Laura, my dear. It is something that women must put up with in order to reap the benefits of marriage. With Aston you had all of the annoyances and none of the benefits, so I can understand why you might feel as you do. But not all men are like Thomas Aston. I promise to find you a nice man who will give you a home and children and buy you pretty things. I promise you won't mind putting up with the indignities of the marital act when you are enjoying its benefits."

The indignities of the marital act. I thought of the way Tom would shove me down on the bed and grind himself into me, all the while squeezing my breasts so that they were bruised and painful for days. He liked hurting me; I could see it in his eyes. When he died I had sworn I would never put myself under the power of a husband again. Buy me pretty things! Never.

That is why owning a boarding school was such a perfect solution to my situation. Rosie could be one of my students. I would own the business and I would never have to depend upon a man to support me and my child ever again.

I could not confide this plan to Aunt Rose, however. She would be horrified, and I did not want to listen to her objections. I said instead, "You'll have a difficult time finding me a husband, Aunt Rose. My parents were gentry, not aristocracy. No one in your social circle is going to want to marry 'the vicar's daughter.' So please don't put yourself to any trouble on my behalf. I like where I am at present and if something changes we can talk then."

She patted my hand. "Something is bound to change, my dear Laura. Robert needs to marry. And quickly. It's imperative that he get an heir. Horrible Harold cannot be allowed to inherit. And when Robert marries, your position here will end. No new wife is going to put up with a beautiful governess whom all the servants adore."

My heart cramped. I told myself it was because I didn't want to leave Chiltern. It could have nothing to do with the thought of the earl getting married.

I said firmly, "Aunt Rose, in your circle I am a nobody."

"Perhaps, but you are a very lovely nobody, my dear. When first you came to Chiltern you looked like a wraith but now you are looking healthy and distractingly beautiful. Your face and your sweet disposition will catch you a husband. I am sure of it."

I didn't answer. All I could do is resist whatever mad scheme she came up with. After all, she couldn't force me to get married again. I would rather live with Papa and his awful wife than do that.

*

Aunt Rose retired to take a nap before dinner and I sought out Mason. "What ought we to do about dinner?" I asked my good friend. "Will Lady Baldock object to eating in the small dining room?"

"I don't think so, my lady. But I fear she will object to the table arrangements."

I was certain she would object to the table arrangements. "What do you suggest we do?"

He frowned. "The situation is a little...delicate."

No one knew that better than I.

"My lady, I think you should sit at the end of the table, opposite his lordship. Mr. Kingston and Lady Baldock will sit in the middle of the table, facing each other."

"You don't think Lady Baldock should sit opposite his lordship?"

He shook his head. 'No. You are the mistress of this house and your place at table should reflect that position. I will inform John of our decision and have the table set thusly."

I wasn't really the mistress of the house, as Mason very well knew, but I was touched by his loyalty and I didn't want to gainsay him. "If you think that would be best?" I said doubtfully.

"I do think that, my lady. And I also think you should gather in the drawing room before dinner. Lady Baldock can be very...nice...in her opinions about what should or should not be done."

I agreed with him. If Aunt Rose complained about any of the arrangements, I would tell her to speak to Mason. I knew she would never insult Mason by questioning his authority. Like the earl, she was very fond of him.

*

I did not see the earl until we met in the drawing room before dinner. He had been apprised of Aunt Rose's arrival by Mason and so knew not to come to the gold salon as usual. Neither Aunt Rose nor Mark had yet come in.

"I hear my aunt has arrived," he said as he sat beside me on one of the ivory brocade sofas.

"She has. I consulted Mason about table seating." I told him about what we had decided.

"Excellent," he said.

I still wasn't sure. "Don't you think Aunt Rose should sit opposite you?"

"Certainly not." His crisp reply sent a ripple of pleasure up my spine. "Mason had it right. You are the mistress of this house and that is your position, not Aunt Rose's." He gave me a charmingly mischievous smile. "She will be perfectly happy looking at Kingston."

I laughed.

When Aunt Rose came into the room a few minutes later we stood. She looked at her nephew and said, "You are too thin, Robert. Haven't you been eating?"

"I have been eating my way through all of Mrs. Minton's meals, Aunt Rose," he replied serenely. "If I keep this up I shall be in danger of becoming fat."

She came all the way into the room and took the elegant silk-upholstered chair that stood at a right angle to our sofa. "I must admit I have been looking forward to one of Mrs. Minton's dinners. My own cook is very good, but no one is as good as Mrs. Minton."

I didn't doubt that. I had put on ten pounds since I first came to Chiltern. It had forced me to dip into my salary to purchase some new garments.

Aunt Rose next looked at me. "Is that the only dinner dress you own, Laura?"

My head snapped up. "Of course not. I have several others."

"They're all equally dreadful," the earl said unexpectedly. "Why don't you take Laura shopping Aunt Rose and buy her some new clothes."

I aimed a glare at him, hurt that he had deserted me. "What do you mean, my clothes are 'dreadful'? I bought them in the village and the seamstress there was very pleasant." I turned back to Aunt Rose. "I gained some weight and so I brought my old dresses to her, thinking she could let them out. But I already had taken them in and it was impossible to let them out again. So I bought some new ones."

"You needed to gain weight, my dear," Aunt Rose replied. You looked like a famine victim when first you came here. Every time I came to visit you have looked better, and now…well now you are perfect. Don't gain any more weight."

"I haven't gained anything in quite a while." I was embarrassed by this discussion of my weight and was seeking desperately for another subject to introduce, when Mark came into the room.

Mark had been away every time Aunt Rose had visited and now both the earl and I watched her face as he approached. When he had reached us I said, "Aunt Rose, may I present Mr. Mark Kingston. He is the steward here at Chiltern Hall."

Aunt Rose held out her hand and Mark bowed over it.

She looked dazzled. Mark in evening dress was especially gorgeous.

He said, "I am happy to make your acquaintance, Lady Baldock."

"Mr. K-Kingston." She nodded regally, but she had stuttered. Definitely. It was a stutter.

I exchanged an amused glance with the earl.

Mason loomed in the door and announced dinner was being served. We stood. The earl offered his arm to Aunt Rose and Mark offered his arm to me. This was another ceremony we had dispensed with when it was just the three of us. Aunt Rose seemed perfectly happy with the seating arrangement that had her looking at Mark and she ate everything that was put on her plate. When the time came for the ladies to retire (another ritual the three of us had dispensed with), she informed the men that she would give them fifteen minutes to drink their port and then she expected them to join us in the drawing room. Mark said, "Of course, Lady Baldock."

The earl looked amused.

Aunt Rose said, "Come along, Laura, you and I have things to discuss."

I followed her with a sinking heart.

Chapter Nine

Aunt Rose and I resumed the seats we had taken before dinner. Mason himself came in to see what we might like to drink. He was always very attentive to Aunt Rose. She ordered wine for the both of us.

I did not want wine. I had drunk quite enough at dinner, but I smiled pleasantly and silently decided I wouldn't drink it. I would have liked some tea, but I remained quiet.

"Robert is right about your clothing." This was Aunt Rose's opening salvo. "You need a completely new wardrobe if you are to catch a husband."

I lifted my ribs and sat as straight as I could. "Aunt Rose, I told you I don't wish to marry again."

"And I told you not to talk nonsense. Think of your daughter, Laura. Do you want her brought up as the 'governess' child?' She will always be second or third or fourth best wherever you might go. And she is such a sweet child. She deserves to be allowed to shine."

That shrewd comment was the main reason I had decided to open a school rather than be a governess. If I were the owner of a school *no one* would be allowed to look down on Rosie.

Aunt Rose was continuing, "Laura, you were an only child and the darling of your parents' lives. You never went to school and lived among a group of girls so you have no idea how cruel they can be. Rosie is doing well here at Chiltern because Margaret is a sweetheart and Elizabeth is too young to realize that Rosie is not as important as she is."

I thought of Elizabeth's quick correction when Rosie had called the earl *Uncle Robert* and winced. Elizabeth was becoming aware, I thought.

It was at this point that the earl and Mark entered the drawing room. The earl resumed his place on the sofa next to me and Mark took his place opposite Aunt Rose. I saw her look at him thoughtfully and prayed she wouldn't dismiss him because he was not family. I would stand up for him if I had to, which I knew would annoy Aunt Rose. Thankfully, she said nothing, and Mason arrived with our wine.

"What will you have, Kingston?" the earl asked.

"Whatever you are having, my lord," he replied. Mark's voice was as easy as the earl's, but I saw how his hand on the chair's arm was white around his knuckles.

"Two brandies, Mason," the earl said.

"Certainly, my lord."

Mason bowed himself out and I decided I might need that glass of wine after all. I took a healthy sip.

The earl introduced a comfortable subject and we talked for a few minutes. The brandy came in and Mason himself put the decanter on the low table before all of our seats. Once the door had closed behind Mason, Aunt Rose looked at the earl and made an announcement.

"I have come here to invite you to a house party at Baldock Hall." This was the name of her country estate. "I have already sent out the invitations informing my friends that the purpose of the party is to introduce my nephew, the new Earl of Chiltern, to the *ton*. I am pleased to report that I have had a number of acceptances already." She lifted a hand in a little wave. "Well, I always have acceptances. One has to be dead or dying to refuse an invitation to one of my house parties."

The earl said, "I am sorry, Aunt Rose, but you will have to make my excuses." His voice was perfectly pleasant, but adamant.

Aunt Rose ignored his interruption and looked at me. "I am also planning to introduce you, Laura, to a selection of possible husbands." She turned to regard the earl. "It will be most important for the *ton* to see that Laura has friends in high places. I am her godmother, so of course I am Laura's friend. But when people understand that she is also a friend of the Earl of Chiltern, she should have no trouble. We will say nothing about her acting as your governess, Robert."

The earl was looking grim. He said, "I have no intention of getting married in the immediate future, Aunt Rose. I have only been home for a little more than a month."

Each word came out like a chip of ice. My heart began to hammer. I had never seen him look as he did right now. I thought it must have been the look he wore when he rode into battle.

Aunt Rose did not quail, however. She simply lifted her eyebrows. "Do you want to see Chiltern pass into the hands of Horrible Harold?"

The earl's face froze. "Surely Harold isn't the next heir."

"He is your Uncle Clarence's eldest son. Your brother has left two little girls. Only you stand between Chiltern and Harold."

"Dear God." He and Aunt Rose looked at each other.

This Harold person must be truly dreadful, I thought.

"Surely there's no urgency for me to wed," the earl said. "I'm perfectly healthy, Aunt Rose."

"Who among us can guarantee that he will be here next week, Robert? Life is fragile. You, of all people, should know that."

The earl drained his brandy glass and poured himself another.

I said, "What makes this Harold so horrible?"

The earl said bitterly, "He's a liar, a drunk, a gambler, a womanizer…". Have I left anything out Aunt Rose?"

"The last I heard he was in danger of getting thrown into Debtor's Prison. He may even have left the country. But if he inherits you can be sure his mother will let him know and he will be let loose on Chiltern."

The earl drained his second glass of brandy and poured himself another.

"I have invited several of the prettiest and most eligible girls in the *ton* to the house party."

The earl stared gloomily into his glass. "I think I'd rather go into battle again."

"Don't be ridiculous, Robert. And don't tell me you haven't any experience with good society. You were in Vienna for the Congress, for heaven's sake. From what I gathered all you did there was socialize!"

"We did. It was exhausting."

"You are a Daubeny, my dear. Your ancestor came over with the Conqueror. Another ancestor refused a dukedom because he didn't like the king. You cannot allow Harold to inherit Chiltern."

The earl stared at his now empty brandy glass. "No, I cannot." He got to his feet. "I will do my duty, Aunt Rose. But I don't have to like it."

When the door had closed behind the earl, Aunt Rose turned to Mark. "I am inviting you to the house party as well, Mr. Kingston. As I mentioned to my nephew, there will be several unattached girls present and he won't be able to entertain all of them. A handsome young man like you will be just the thing to keep them occupied."

Mark's composure in the face of this rude invitation was impressive. "Thank you, Lady Baldock," he said. "I should be honored to attend your house party."

"Good. That is settled then. The invitation is for the third week in September, but I would like you all to arrive a day early."

"Yes, Aunt Rose," I said.

"Yes, Lady Baldock," Mark said.

Aunt Rose stood up. "I believe I will retire."

Mark and I jumped up as well.

"Breakfast will be laid out in the small dining room, as usual," I said.

"Good night, my darling Laura." She leaned over to kiss my cheek. "Just follow my advice and all will be well."

"Yes, Aunt Rose." But as she walked to the door I thought, *I will go to this party, but I will not find a husband.*

Mark said, "I didn't know you were looking for a husband, Laura." His face was whiter than usual and he looked strained.

I said, "I am definitely *not* looking for a husband, Mark. This party of Aunt Rose's will be a futile exercise for my part of her plan."

"You can't remain at Chiltern forever, Laura," he pointed out. "Eventually you will need to make some arrangement for your future."

"I know," I replied. "But marriage isn't one of my choices." I stood up. "I think I am going to retire as well. I will see you in the morning, Mark."

"Sleep well," Mark said.

Not likely, I thought, but I smiled at him, said "You too," and followed Aunt Rose out of the room.

Chapter Ten

As I soon discovered, the *ton* began throwing house parties in August, when the shooting season opened. From then to the opening of Parliament they entertained themselves by hosting and visiting parties at various Great Houses. As Aunt Rose modestly told us, she (her husband the earl was rarely mentioned) was famous for the house party she hosted every year on the third week in September.

The morning after her invitation/demand was issued, I found Aunt Rose sitting at the breakfast table with Mark when I came in. I had missed my morning ride with the earl because I had overslept. This was because I had spent most of the night worrying about this wretched house party.

Both wished me good morning and Mark excused himself saying he had an appointment. Before I even sat down Aunt Rose fixed me with a determined gaze. "We have only a few weeks to get you ready to make your entrance into society, Laura," she said.

I made a final stab at freedom. "I'll be out of my depth with your friends, Aunt Rose. It is very nice of you to invite me, but I don't think it's a good idea."

"My darling Laura." She smiled at me, a genuinely tender smile, and my heart sank. How could I deny her when she thought she was being so good to me? "There is a quality about you, a warmth, that shines in those big brown eyes of yours. You have no idea how lovely you are, do you?"

I could feel myself flush. "You are too kind," I murmured in embarrassment.

Mercifully Aunt Rose changed the subject. "You have nothing to worry about, my dear girl. I have everything in hand. You and I, and that magnificent young man, Mr. Kingston, are going into London on Monday to order clothes. Robert has a perfectly adequate wardrobe from his days in Vienna but he says he has business at the Horse Guards. He wants to see his banker as well, so he will be coming too. It shouldn't take us more than a week. No one is in town and the modistes will be glad to have work."

I protested that I shouldn't leave the children. After all, I was being paid to look after them.

"The children can have a vacation from their schooling and they will be perfectly safe with Nana," Aunt Rose returned.

Since I knew she was right, there was nothing else I could think of to object to.

She went back to her own substantial breakfast, and I stood at the table loaded with breakfast food and looked at her in bewilderment. How had this happened? How had Aunt Rose come to have such authority over my life? Over all our lives? I wanted to protest once more that I liked it here at Chiltern, but she had said some things I couldn't forget for the simple reason that she was right.

I had been the de facto mistress of Chiltern for a year, and I knew I would hate seeing another woman in my place. Especially a woman who was married to the earl.

I would hate that most of all.

I brought a plate of food to the table and sat across from her. I asked curiously, "Are you going to pay for Mark's clothes too?"

"Certainly not. That would be highly inappropriate. He has assured me that he is perfectly capable of purchasing his own clothing."

I wondered if Mark's great aunt had died. He had said nothing to me about coming into his inheritance. However, if that was the case, then perhaps Mark would find a wife at Aunt Rose's party!

The thought of the three of us coming home engaged to be married should have been amusing but for some reason I didn't find it at all funny.

*

The day before we left for London I went riding with the earl. We had not ridden together since Aunt Rose arrived, and I was thrilled when I saw him wearing his riding clothes and talking to Walsh. With Aunt Rose at the table, we had not been able to talk as freely as we were accustomed to, and I looked forward to spending some time alone with him.

Beau was saddled and ready when I made my appearance and the earl said he would wait for Cachet to be saddled as well. It didn't take long before the mare was led out of the stable. We both mounted and, with mutual if unspoken agreement, headed toward the trail that would take us down to the lake.

The earl didn't speak as we rode across the park, and I peeked sideways at his profile, wondering whether I should be the one to break the silence. He turned as if he had felt my look and said, "If Aunt Rose was in the army she would be the Commander-in-Chief by now. Wellington wouldn't have stood a chance against her."

I laughed. "Was she always like this?"

"I don't know how she was with my father and my brother, but she was always very good to me. George was the heir and he got all the attention. Aunt Rose always tried to make me feel as if I was important too."

"She was good to me as well. Every time she came to visit it was like a party. She would bring presents and delicious treats. She and my mother were like sisters. My father thought she was too worldly, but he always welcomed her for my mother's sake."

We rode for a bit. Then I said, "What kind of man is her husband?"

I heard the amusement in his voice. "He is very good at saying, 'Yes, my dear; of course, my dear; anything you want, my dear.'"

"A perfect husband for Aunt Rose."

"He's quite a nice old fellow. Fifteen years older than Rose."

"She never spoke of children."

"She had one son, who died when he was very young. The heir to the earldom is a nephew who is far more responsible than Harold."

I felt sad. "Poor Aunt Rose. It seems we received the love she couldn't give to her own child."

"You are a very perceptive young woman." His voice was so quiet that I had to move Cachet closer to Beau to hear him.

"Sometimes," I said. "I wasn't very perceptive when I chose my husband."

As soon as those words were spoken I wished them back. I did not want to talk about Tom. I had put him behind me and I had no idea why I had dragged him into this conversation.

"Aunt Rose said something about him being a bit of a bounder."

Thank God his voice was neutral. If it had been full of sympathy I couldn't have borne it.

"A bit," I said.

He didn't reply and we had to split up to go down the steep hill that led to the lake. The earl went first and I divided my attention between the ground in front of us, which Cachet knew as well as I did, and the man in front of me. He was so slim that one didn't expect his shoulders to be as broad as they were.

When I was able to move up beside him again I asked, "May I ask what your business is at the Horse Guards or is it secret?"

"It's not a secret," he said. "They want me to go to Paris to help Wellington establish order. I am not going, however. I am needed here. An estate the size of this one needs the owner's attention if it is to run properly."

I was delighted to hear this. I had been concerned that he might be sent on some mission, and I agreed with his reason for refusing. Chiltern needed him.

"Aunt Rose makes an odd sort of cupid," I said, as we turned onto the trail that would take us around the lake.

His face, which had been relaxed, tightened. "If only my cousin Harold wasn't the heir. I have known nothing but men and war since I was eighteen years old. I'm not ready to get married yet."

"Neither am I!" The words burst out of me. "I hated being married!"

He looked down at me from Beau, a surprised look on his face.

"Let's canter," I said abruptly and squeezed Cachet's side with my calf. She threw up her head and, when I kept up the pressure, exploded into a canter. Beau was quick to follow, and the two horses cantered briskly around the lake. When we came back to a walk the earl introduced another topic and we finished our ride in easy accord.

Chapter Eleven

We stayed at Chiltern House, which was on Grosvenor Square, one of the "best addresses in London" according to Aunt Rose. Grosvenor Square was attractive enough, with a line of mostly brown brick buildings with red dressings grouped around a large formal garden. Number twelve, the earl's house, was one of the brown brick buildings

I had traveled in the Chiltern coach with Aunt Rose and Mark; the earl had driven his phaeton. We left Chiltern early and arrived in London by late afternoon. Mason was at the door to greet us. He had left Chiltern Hall the previous day along with Mrs. Minton and several other servants. Chiltern House did not keep a full staff when no one was in residence.

We walked into a lovely entrance hall and Mason summoned two of the waiting footmen to fetch our baggage. I smiled at Luke and Andrew as they passed by.

"I think this house just might do for us," Mark murmured to me humorously as we stood listening to Aunt Rose confer with Mason.

"Possibly," I replied with assumed hauteur.

Aunt Rose said, "Mason tells me that Robert has already arrived. He is in the stable seeing to his horses. I suggest we go upstairs to wash and change our clothing for dinner. We dine at seven."

Mark and I obediently followed Aunt Rose to a narrow staircase and we ascended. Mason followed to point out the rooms to which Aunt Rose had assigned Mark and me.

My room was painted a pretty pale yellow, and the bed and the two chairs in front of the tile fireplace looked comfortable. Best of all, May was waiting for me.

May was the closest thing I had to a lady's maid. She looked in on me every morning to help button up my gowns and she helped me out of them when I needed to change clothes. She was young and pretty and we liked each other.

"Have you ever been to London before, May?" I asked.

"No, my lady." Her blue eyes were wide. "Mason said Luke and Andrew and I could take a few hours tomorrow in the afternoon to look around the city. Is it possible for me to go with them? Of course, if you need me here...."

Her blue eyes were begging me. I picked up my purse and took some money out. "Take this. Have a good time."

"Oh no, my lady! Mason said he would give the boys some money."

Bravo Mason, I thought.

I smiled and said, "Keep it. Perhaps you will see something you would like to purchase."

Her cheeks were pink with pleasure. "Thank you, my lady. You are very kind."

There was a knock on the door and when May opened it Luke came in with my bags. "I hear you are taking a tour of London tomorrow afternoon," I said to him.

"Yes, my lady." Luke was a nice-looking young man in his twenties. I admonished him to take good care of May.

"Of course, my lady!" He looked at May and smiled. She blushed.

Luke left and May unpacked my bags. "What dress do you want for this evening, my lady?"

I had brought one evening gown with me, two morning frocks and two day dresses. They were well-worn but they were appropriate. Aunt Rose had seen them all and disapproved.

Dinner was simpler than the dinners we had at home, but it was very good. I don't think Mrs. Minton was capable of producing a bad meal. Aunt Rose discoursed about what dressmakers we should visit tomorrow and, when Mark asked, the earl told him the name of his tailor. "The men of my family have always gone to Stultz," he said.

"And to Hoby for boots," Aunt Rose put in with authority.

The earl met my eyes and we both smothered a smile. Aunt Rose had an opinion on absolutely everything.

We were tired from the long ride and went to bed early. I might be defensive about my clothing but I must confess I was very much looking forward to something new!

*

We bought or ordered everything imaginable that a woman could want and far more than she would need. We bought morning dresses, carriage dresses, afternoon dresses, walking dresses, dinner gowns, ball gowns, a soft white wool wrap, silk stockings, kid leather shoes, brown leather half-boots, chemises, parasols, gloves, hats, and a new riding habit.

I protested that Aunt Rose was buying me far more than I would need for a week at her house. She replied that she was buying me my trousseau and that it was my wedding gift.

"I'm not married yet, Aunt Rose!" I wanted to stamp my foot like a child I was so frustrated. "I may never be married. I'm not precisely what your friends would call a 'suitable wife'."

"You will find a husband, my dear. I am certain of it."

Of course I was grateful to her, for caring for me, for spending so much money on me. But I also felt indebted. She wanted me to find a husband and I was beginning to feel as if I owed it to her to attach one.

Mark had been as shocked as I at the price of clothing. I was worried that he hadn't enough money, but he assured me the charges hadn't drained all of his resources. "Great Aunt Lizzie passed away a month ago and the bank agreed to pay my expenses for the house party."

I found it strange that he hadn't told me about his aunt's death, but perhaps he didn't want it to seem as if he were happy she died. "Perhaps *you'll* find a wife at this house party," I said.

He shook his head and laughed.

This conversation took place just as Mark and I were approaching the Tower of London. The earl was spending the day

69

at the Horse Guards and Aunt Rose was visiting an old friend, so Mark and I had decided to tour London. Both of us had been here once, on quick visits with our parents, but we had never seen the Tower of London.

We were walking in the main gate when I recognized the couple approaching us. They were holding hands and talking intently to each other.

"Isn't that one of the footmen?" Mark said.

"Yes." And the girl was my lady's maid, May.

The two of them were so involved with each other they would have passed us by if I hadn't said loudly, "May! Luke! How nice to see you. Are you enjoying your visit to London?"

They dropped hands and looked at me like guilty things surprised.

Luke was the first to find his tongue. "Yes, we have been seeing as much as we can."

"Yes." This was May's contribution to the conversation.

"But where is Andrew?" I looked over Luke's shoulder as if I expected Andrew to miraculously appear.

"He decided not to come," Luke said. His face was flushed.

"I see." I regarded him in silence. With the white powder of a footman washed out of his blond hair, Luke was an extremely good-looking young man. He was tall—all of Chiltern's footmen had to be tall—and broad shouldered. I looked at my pretty little maid and thought, *Be careful May. Don't ruin your life over this boy.*

As the daughter of a vicar I had seen this sort of thing too often. A pretty young girl and a handsome young man, and then a baby, whom neither of them was capable of supporting. They weren't even capable of supporting themselves, so marriage wasn't a possibility. When this situation happened at home, Papa would talk to the girl's parents to try to get them to keep their daughter and her baby. If the parents refused there was a place where girls could go and have their baby, but the baby had to be given up. I always

thought it horribly cruel and I couldn't bear to see my little May in such a situation.

I forced a smile and bade them good day, but I couldn't appreciate the historically famous Tower as we walked around it. My mind was preoccupied with May. I would have a talk with her when we got back to the house.

*

The earl seemed preoccupied over dinner. Aunt Rose asked him how his appointment at the Horse Guards had gone and his response had been a noncommittal, "All right." Before we retired for the night, however, he asked me if I would like to drive in the park the following morning.

"I am missing our morning rides," he said.

"I would very much like to go for a drive," I said. "I am missing our rides as well."

*

Since the Season was over and the *ton* had left London, the park was almost empty. The earl threaded his way through the busy London streets and we entered the park from Oxford Street. We were both seated on the high seat of the phaeton and I felt the closeness of his body in a way that was unnerving me. Surreptitiously I move a little away.

"You didn't seem very happy about your trip to the Horse Guards," I said tentatively. I didn't usually venture a comment on anything that might be his private affair.

"I tendered my formal resignation," he said. "They weren't happy. They thought I was just the person to head up their intelligence section. They were 'counting on me,' they said. No one else could do it as well as I. They spouted a lot of nonsense like that."

I digested this in silence. Then I said cautiously, "Intelligence. Doesn't that mean spying?"

He shot me a glance. "Among other things."

Indignation flared in my chest. How dare they try to manipulate him? A man who had given eight years of his young life to his country! I looked at his beautifully chiseled profile and said, "If they tried to make you feel guilty about leaving, then shame on them. You fought for your country for eight years. You have every right to take up your own life again."

He shot me a look, raised a black eyebrow and said with amusement, "You should have come with me, Laura."

"I would have given those men a piece of my mind. You have an enormous estate to run and thousands of people depend upon you for their livelihoods. You have two little girls who need a parent. How could they possibly think you would agree to their offer?"

He didn't reply and we drove for a while in silence. Neither of us was ever uncomfortable with silence. I looked around and enjoyed the park.

"I thought there would be more carriages about," I said.

"According to Aunt Rose this road is packed during the Season. I'm sure most Londoners are thrilled when the Season is over and all the aristocrats have left the city to its true citizens."

We drove for a little more and he asked me a question about one of the tenant's families at Chiltern. We spent the remainder of the drive talking about home.

Chapter Twelve

We stayed in London for four days. At the end of that time some of my wardrobe was finished and the rest could be sent on to Chiltern Hall when it was finished. We were all eager to get home, even Aunt Rose. She said London was boring outside of the Season; according to her the teeming city was empty.

We departed for home early on a gray overcast morning. After an hour of riding in the carriage Aunt Rose fell asleep, which gave Mark and me a chance to talk. I asked him about how his family had taken the news of his inherited wealth, and for the first time he talked about them. As he talked it occurred to me that although I had spent many hours conversing with Mark, I really didn't know much about him.

His father was a deeply religious man who had little time for his six sons. His mother did the best she could, but his father was only interested in his parish church. It had been built in the Middle Ages and, unfortunately, it had not been kept up by previous vicars and was sorely in need of repairs. Mark said his father's mission in life was to restore the church to its former glory, and to this end he poured all of his money into its restoration. His six sons were left to figure out their own futures. There was a distinct note of bitterness in Mark's voice as he said that last sentence.

"I was the fortunate one," Mark said. "My great aunt paid my tuition at Eton. My two eldest brothers joined the army, my third brother joined the navy and my other two brothers managed to marry women who were decently situated."

I wondered how he had fared at Eton, a mere vicar's son in that bastion of the aristocracy. "Did you like Eton?" I asked tentatively.

He got a tight look on his face. "I did at first."

At first. I wondered what he meant by that, but it would be prying to ask. He must have seen the look on my face because he added, "I was good at sports and I was smart. Eton was fine, Laura. I got a good education there."

I was touched by his story. *How many boys like Mark are there in England? I thought. Intelligent boys whose abilities are never recognized because they do not have the right "connections."*

I asked, "What would you do if you had your own choice of the future?"

He replied instantly. "I'd like to sit in the Commons."

I had not expected that answer. "The Commons?"

"Yes. The Commons are the only place a man of undistinguished social standing can make a career for himself, can become someone important, someone of standing in the world."

I had never guessed that Mark had political aspirations. I said, "Perhaps the earl can help you."

Before Mark could answer, Aunt Rose woke up. She said something to Mark, and as they chatted I realized why Mark had spent so much money on clothing. He was probably hoping to make some contacts at the house party, the kind of contacts that were so important to a young man who wanted to go into politics.

*

When we arrived back at Chiltern Hall the first thing I did was run up the stairs to the nursery. I had only been away from Rosie for four days, but it seemed an eternity. I walked into the big room just as Mary Anne was serving the pudding. Rosie saw me first and screamed, *"Mama, you're home!"* She pushed her chair back and came running to greet me. "I missed you!" she cried and locked her arms around my waist.

I bent to plant a kiss on the top of her soft curls. "Have they been torturing you?"

She looked up at me, her big brown eyes smiling. "No."

Margaret came over to greet me too. "We all missed you, Lady Laura. It's not the same when you're not here."

I pried Rosie away from me and bestowed a hug on Margaret. She hugged me back with almost as much passion as Rosie had.

Elizabeth was standing behind Margaret and she was smiling as well. "Would you like to give me a hug too?" I asked her.

I was a little surprised, and very gratified, when she said gruffly, "Yes. It's boring here when you're not around." And she put her arms around me and squeezed.

I had bought some new puzzles in London for the nursery and Margaret and Elizabeth were eager to try to solve them. The puzzles were too old for Rosie but I had other things for her. A new doll—she loved dolls—and paints. She loved to paint. She made a mess, but she surprised me with how good her pictures were. It was a talent I wanted to encourage.

*

It seemed as if we had just come home when we needed to pack again to go to Baldock Hall for Aunt Rose's house party. She had given us a list of the people who would be there and I was utterly intimidated. The earl just shrugged—he was an aristocrat himself and even if he didn't know these people he would feel perfectly comfortable among them. I didn't feel the same way. I was of the gentry and might be regarded as a lady, but these people were out of my reach.

Before she left for Baldock Hall to prepare for the house party Aunt Rose had given me a list of four young men she considered potential suitors for my hand.

"Frank Lovejoy is a possible choice. He is a nephew of the Earl of Arlington and I understand he made quite a lot of money in the exchange. He is in his early thirties and was quite visible during the Season. I think he's looking for a wife."

Aunt Rose and I were sitting in the blue salon the night before her departure. She had announced she needed to speak to me privately and this was the room she chose. It wasn't a room I was particularly fond of—the paintings were very gloomy.

Aunt Rose and I were sitting side by side on the blue brocade sofa and she had a list in her hand. She had actually made a list for me so I would know whom I should try to impress.

"Richard Fenwick is the second son of the Earl of Hawkmoor but he's rather more plump in the pocket than most second sons. He inherited a nice estate from an uncle, and I hear it has quite a decent income. You like living in the country; he might suit you perfectly, Laura.

"John Emmott is a cousin of Viscount Ridley. He has a small estate in Somerset and has inherited a castle in Scotland from his mother. He is the least wealthy of the lot—his money is from his Scottish grandfather—but I think you would like him.

"Then there is Lord Castlewood, heir to the Duke of Mandavile. I invited him but I don't know if he will show any interest in you, my dear. Lady Mary Winstanley, a diamond of the first order who was the Incomparable of this year's Season, refused at least four other offers because she was waiting for him. He didn't come up to scratch, however, and I understand she was furious. He's here for the shooting, but you might make an impression on him, Laura."

I said very little as Aunt Rose went through this terrifying list of names. I would never "catch" any of these men, but I knew if I said that to Aunt Rose she would brush my objections aside. I was going to have to go through this pitiful charade before she understood that a vicar's daughter, who had a child and not a penny to her name, would not be considered as a possible wife by any of these men.

It was early but I didn't join the others in the drawing room. I was too upset. I did not want to go to this party, but I owed it to Aunt Rose to attend. She had been so good to me—visiting and bringing me presents when I was a child, and finding me this position after Tom died. I had to make at least a pretense of trying to attach a husband.

I took a candle from the table at the bottom of the stairs and started to climb. I met the earl on the second floor; he was coming down as I was going up.

"Going to bed so early?" he asked.

We both were holding candles and the flickering light threw shadows on his face. "Yes," I said gloomily.

"By any chance did you have a little talk with Aunt Rose?"

"I did." My voice was even gloomier. "She has four men I am supposed to hunt down at this party."

"I have four girls who have been invited to hunt me."

He didn't sound gloomy at all. He sounded resigned.

"Oh." This was my brilliant reply.

He looked down at me. The candlelight made his lashes look very long and his cheekbones more prominent. My heart skipped a beat. I knew there was a part of him that he kept to himself, and I wanted so much for him to share it with me. I looked at his mouth and thought I wouldn't mind at all if *he* wanted to kiss me.

This treacherous thought reverberated throughout my body and I almost gasped with shock.

I wet my lips with my tongue. "Th-thank you, my lord. And now I think I had better be getting along to my room."

He stood aside to let me pass and I almost ran up the stairs to the nursery.

I had met the only man I wanted to marry, but he was further out of my reach than anyone on Aunt Rose's list. The thought was like a stab to my heart. He was as far above my reach as...as.... A few lines from Shakespeare popped into my head:

> *It were all one*
> *That I should love a bright particular star*
> *And think to wed it, he is so above me.*

I was his employee. I knew he liked me. He was grateful for my care of the children. He enjoyed my company. But I had heard Aunt Rose's words, the words that had convinced him that he must marry. The Daubeny family was entwined with the history of this country. He was expected to marry a girl of noble birth. It would never even cross his mind that he might marry his employee. Nor had it crossed Aunt Rose's mind that I might be a suitable candidate to be her nephew's countess. She did love me, but my rank wasn't elevated enough for the Earl of Chiltern.

May was waiting for me and conversing with her distracted me for a little while. Then I was in my nightgown; then I was in bed; then I cried myself to sleep. I truly thought my heart would break.

Chapter Thirteen

Baldock Hall, Aunt Rose's home, was one of Robert Adam's acclaimed masterpieces. It was absolutely lovely. I loved the colors—the delicate pinks, grays, blues and greens. I loved the arches filled with classical sculpture. I loved the fabulous paintings. But it didn't have the same feeling as Chiltern had—that feeling of one family having lived there for centuries, the feeling of rootedness.

I hadn't realized it until now, but I had grown to appreciate Chiltern during the time I lived there. I still didn't like those frigid looking salons, but I had settled into the safety of its permanence, its feeling of family.

The three of us—the earl, Mark and I—had shared the carriage ride. It was only a few hours to Aunt Rose's estate and the men talked business. The earl had questions about some of the properties he owned, and I thought Mark sounded strangely defensive as he answered them. I could feel the tension between the two men and I wondered where it had come from. They had always seemed to get along so well.

When we arrived at Baldock Hall Aunt Rose herself met us at the door with her husband beside her. His appearance was a shock. I knew he was older than she, but he was *old*. His face and neck were a mass of wrinkles. Aunt Rose looked like a girl beside him.

He greeted the earl effusively. Mark and I got a more tepid reception. Then Aunt Rose whisked us away to our bedrooms. The earl was on the second floor; Mark and I were on the third. Aunt Rose told us that our baggage had arrived earlier along with my maid and the earl's valet.

She said to Mark, "One of the footmen can assist you, Mr. Kingston. I understand you have not brought a valet."

Mark assured her that he was capable of dressing himself. "Good," she replied, and whisked herself away leaving us standing in front of the doors that had our names posted on them.

"I'll knock on your door when I'm ready," Mark said. "We can go down together."

I thought this was an excellent idea and promised I would be ready by 6:45.

*

Forty of us sat down to dinner at seven. Aunt Rose had been apologetic about the early hour. Apparently it was fashionable to dine at eight—or even nine—but her husband preferred to eat at seven. I perfectly understood him. Old people didn't like to eat late in the evening. It wasn't good for their digestion. And it didn't discommode me at all—at Chiltern we always ate at seven.

I was placed a third of the way down the enormous table that filled the dining room. Mark was a few places away, with two elderly women on either side of him. They looked delighted. He looked nervous. The earl was close to Aunt Rose and seated beside him was one of the loveliest girls I had ever seen. She had golden hair and porcelain skin and she looked like an angel. I thought that she must be the Lady Mary Winstanley Aunt Rose had talked about, the one who was holding out for a title and whom she was inviting as a "possible" for the earl. I took her in instant dislike.

The earl's head turned, as if he had felt my gaze, and for a brief moment we looked at each other across the table. I thought he looked a little grim. I felt a little grim myself, but I hoped it wasn't showing on my face.

Aunt Rose had placed a prospective suitor on either side of me. Richard Fenwick, the second son of the Earl of Hawkmoor, politely turned to me while we were awaiting the first course and said, "I'm so sorry, but in the crush in the drawing room I didn't get your name."

"I am Lady Laura Aston, my lord," I answered. "Lady Baldock is my godmother."

He lifted an eyebrow and said, "Are all her goddaughters as pretty as you?"

I smiled at the compliment and asked him if he lived in London.

"For part of the time I do. I have rooms on St. James Street. But this is my favorite time of year. The shooting season has opened and in a month it will be cold enough to hunt."

"You sound as if you're quite a sportsman," I said.

For the remainder of the time he had my attention I listened to detailed descriptions of his favorite sports. I had never understood the charm of shooting birds. They were shot in such large numbers each day that it was impossible for them all to be eaten. They had been killed for no reason beyond the fun of it. I am quite fond of birds and I didn't approve.

I had experienced hunting only a few times. My father did not approve of hunting, and I only got a chance to join the local hunt when the squire specifically invited me. I loved it. The feel of riding a horse at full gallop over field after field, jumping whatever obstacle might be in your path, the baying of the hounds as they found a scent—it was glorious! I felt vaguely sorry for the poor fox who had given us such a wonderful run, but I conveniently put that to the back of my mind. I would hunt every day if I could.

The meal was delicious and took a long time to serve. When we were halfway through the menu Mr. Fenwick said, "I deeply regret having to leave your charming company, Lady Aston, but it is time for me to speak to the lady on my other side."

I was familiar with this practice and for the last few minutes had been wondering when I would be rid of Mr. Fenwick and his sporting talk. The moment came, and nearly everyone at the table turned to the person who sat to their left.

I sneaked a quick glance at Mark before I turned. The elderly lady he had been speaking to was beaming and the new recipient of his magnificence was regarding him with wonder. I smothered a smile and turned to greet the man seated on my left, an elderly gentleman who told me his wife was a cousin of Aunt Rose. Lord Brentford asked me if I liked opera, and when I told him I had never seen one, he proceeded to tell me the story of what had to be every opera ever written, along with the names of all their great arias.

I was relieved when dinner was over and the ladies moved back into the drawing room while the gentleman settled down to drink port and talk politics.

*

I awoke at my usual time and May was there to help me into a pretty pale-yellow morning gown. One of Aunt Rose's gifts. I went downstairs and a footman directed me to the room where breakfast was laid out. I stopped when I reached the doorway and felt a flash of panic. The room was filled with men.

I took a quick look around and saw that neither the earl nor Mark was among them. I was beginning to back away and return to my room when a feminine voice called, "Come in, Lady Aston, and join me. I'm glad to see I'm not the only female who doesn't lie around in bed for half the day."

The owner of the voice was seated halfway down the table and had a plate of food in front of her. As most of the men were standing, the seat next to her was open. The room began to empty as I made my way towards her.

I sat down and said with deep sincerity, "Thank you for saving me. Why are there no ladies present?" As she raised her arched brown eyebrow, I added hastily, "Except you, of course...." I hesitated in embarrassment. I didn't know her name and I could feel my face growing warm.

She smiled and said, "I am Lady Matcham. We didn't get a chance to speak last evening. You are Rose's goddaughter I believe."

Lady Matcham was a nice-looking woman with the blue eyes and light hair one so often sees in England. She looked as if she might be in her forties. I replied, "Yes. She was kind enough to invite me. Are the men going shooting? Is that why they were all here for breakfast?"

"Yes. The grouse season has just opened and half the males on this island are heading outdoors with a gun."

Without thinking I said, "Poor grouse."

"Don't say that here," Lady Matcham warned. There was no humor in her face or voice as she spoke. "Shooting grouse is a sacred thing to the men you just saw."

At Lady Matcham's urging I filled my plate with a thick slice of ham, a scoop of eggs and some buttered toast. She had finished her meal by the time I returned with mine but to my relief she showed no signs of leaving.

I put the plate of food and cup of hot tea down and resumed my seat. "May I ask you a question?"

"Of course."

"What do we women do while the men are out shooting birds?"

"We do whatever it pleases us to do. Would you like to take a walk with me after breakfast? The grounds are really beautiful."

"I would love to take a walk with you," I said gratefully.

We chatted companionably while I ate and she drank another cup of tea. I made arrangements to meet with her in the morning room for our walk. "Wear boots," she warned as she left me on the landing.

I wondered for a moment if I should knock at Mark's door and ask if he would like to join our walk. He was as out of his element here as I was. But then, he might still be sleeping and I didn't want to wake him. I went into my room to change my shoes.

*

Lady Matcham was a no-nonsense sort of person. She reminded me of Fanny Beecham who ran the Ladies Guild at my father's church. Once my mind had made that comparison, I relaxed and enjoyed Lady Matcham's company and the day.

The grounds were indeed beautiful. We chose a path that Lady Matcham called the woodland walk. The woods that bordered both sides of this path were extremely beautiful. At one point a small river ran alongside the path as it slanted downward. A series of small waterfalls added to the attractiveness of the scene, and when we stopped descending we were on the shore of a large lake.

Two men were fishing in the lake. One of them was Lady Matcham's nephew.

"Hallo there!" she called as we came down to the lakeside. "Have you caught anything, John?"

Her nephew turned to look at her. I looked at the back of the man with him and my heart jumped inside my chest. I would know that black hair and those shoulders anywhere. It was the earl.

Lady Matcham's nephew put his rod down and began to advance toward us. "Aunt Maud! Out for a walk I see."

Lady Matcham took my elbow and steered me toward the grassy slope that led to the lake. "I have someone here I want you to meet," she said to her approaching nephew.

The earl had also put down his rod and was coming up the grassy slope behind Lady Matcham's nephew.

"Good morning, my lord," Lady Matcham said to the earl.

"Good morning, Lady Matcham," he replied, coming up to stand next to me. He turned his head, looked down at me and said, "Are you having a pleasant walk, Lady Aston?"

He was dressed in casual buckskin trousers and he had taken off his coat to fish. His shirt was open at the throat showing some of his neck, and a lock of his hair had fallen across his forehead. "Y-yes," I stuttered in reply. "Very pleasant."

Lady Matcham took my hand and brought me closer to her side. "Lady Aston, I would like to introduce Mr. John Emmott."

I tore my eyes from the earl and looked at her nephew, who was on Aunt Rose's list. He was pleasant enough looking with brown hair and ordinary blue eyes. His nose had a bump in the middle, as if he had broken it sometime in the past. I held out my hand and he bowed over it. "I am very pleased to meet you, Lady Aston."

I smiled. "It is a pleasure to meet you, Mr. Emmott. Lady Matcham tells me you are her nephew."

He shot a fond look at my companion then returned his eyes to me. "I am fortunate indeed to be Lady Matcham's nephew."

"Lady Aston is Lady Baldock's goddaughter, John," Lady Matcham said.

"Indeed?" The young man looked at me with curiosity. "I wondered why we haven't we met before, my lady. Have you been hiding in the country?"

I produced a smile and tried to think how I should reply. I was still standing silent when the earl said easily, "Lady Aston was widowed last year. She came to my rescue when I had to leave England to go to Vienna. My Aunt Rose convinced her to move into Chiltern Hall and act as its chatelaine while I was gone. I did not like to leave it unsupervised for so many months."

"Indeed?" Mr. Emmott looked at me curiously.

"I am of course moving back to my father's house now that Lord Chiltern has returned." I parroted the response Aunt Rose had insisted I make if anyone inquired about my living arrangements.

The earl looked at the sky. "It's getting a bit late to catch fish, Emmott. Shall we accompany the ladies on their walk?"

"As long as I can walk with Lady Aston," Mr. Emmott replied.

"Of course," the earl replied amiably.

I looked at the bucket under the tree. "What about the fish?"

The earl went over to the bucket, picked it up, walked down to the lake and dumped its contents into the water.

I stared at him in surprise as he returned to our group.

He looked at me and shrugged. "They weren't the kind of fish people like to eat."

Mr. Emmott looked surprised but said nothing. The earl retrieved his jacket from the grass and we continued on our walk. Mr. Emmott and I went first on the trail and Lady Matcham and the earl walked behind us. I thought this a very unsatisfactory arrangement and gave only half my attention to Mr. Emmott. He didn't seem to notice, or if he did, he didn't mind. He seemed a nice man but I wanted to be walking next to the earl.

By the time we reached home a luncheon had been set out in the same dining room as breakfast. Aunt Rose was there and she absolutely beamed when she saw me walk in with Mr. Emmott. I wanted to roll my eyes, but resisted the urge. A soft voice behind us said, "Did you enjoy the shooting this morning, Lord Chiltern?"

I turned a little to get a glance at who was talking to the earl. It was the blonde girl from last night's dinner.

Don't pay any mind to her. I sent this thought to the earl. *She only wants your title and to be mistress of Chiltern. She doesn't care about you.*

The Earl did not appear to have heard my silent appeal because he bent his head and said something to her. She laughed up at him and he smiled.

I turned away. It hurt too much to watch him with another woman.

Chapter Fourteen

The next few days were similar to the first. I shot archery on the lawn one morning, played croquet on another and went for a carriage ride with some of the young ladies on the third. They were distant but polite and I was the same. Of course I hated every one of them; they were the ones picked by Aunt Rose to be candidates for the earl's hand.

After we had got through the morning and the men had returned, luncheon was available in the dining room. It was an informal meal, much like breakfast. You filled your plate from a table groaning with every kind of food imaginable and sat where there was an empty seat. Two out of the three days I saw the earl come in with Lady Margaret Fleetwood, the heiress who had missed the Season because she was in mourning for her brother who had been killed in France. She was quite a pretty girl with silvery blonde hair and hazel eyes. She was also the daughter of an earl. A perfect match I thought bitterly as I watched the earl's dark head bend to listen to something she was saying.

Mr. Frank Lovejoy, one of Aunt Rose's possibles, was behind me at the food table and asked if he could sit next to me. I forced myself to smile at him and say, "Of course."

The earl and Lady Margaret took seats further down the table. He never glanced my way once. I could almost feel my heart breaking inside my chest.

Mr. Lovejoy asked if he could show me the gardens after luncheon and, apathetically, I agreed.

According to Aunt Rose, Mr. Lovejoy was quite rich. He was not a model of masculine beauty, however. He was so thin he looked as if a gust of wind would blow him over. His blond hair was already receding and he wasn't much taller than me. I scolded myself for judging him on his looks, but upon further acquaintance I discovered his personality was as uninspiring as his looks.

The two of us spent the afternoon walking along the circular path, which wound through the traditionally formal gardens of Baldock Hall. I was truly amazed by what I saw. Our surroundings started out much as I expected; there was a lake, a waterfall and beautiful flowers and shrubbery. Then we came around a turn and I found myself staring at a scene that was straight out of ancient Rome. There was a full-sized Roman arch and colonnade, with busts of prominent Romans arranged in the colonnade arches. It was awe inspiring. As we walked on I saw scene after scene of ancient Rome, each of them arranged between the traditional flow of the gardens.

Mr. Lovejoy had an enormous amount of information about each individual setting. He was very interesting, and I was glad I had accepted his invitation. I was actually enjoying myself until the moment we sat together on one of the benches that were scattered along the path and he began to question me.

Who was my father? Who was my mother? Was I in debt because of Sir Thomas' gaming losses? Why was I living at Chiltern Hall? Why was I still there now that the earl was home?

I answered his questions exactly as Aunt Rose had instructed me: My father was a vicar and my mother was the daughter of a baronet. Lord Castlereagh had asked the earl to represent Great Britain at the Congress and my godmother had approached me about moving to Chiltern Hall. The earl did not feel comfortable leaving the house and his two young nieces to the sole supervision of the servants; he needed someone to act as a chatelaine. Since Aunt Rose could not leave her own home, she had asked me if I would undertake this responsibility. I concluded this speech by saying I had taken the temporary position in order to help Aunt Rose, but now that the earl had returned, my daughter and I would be removing to my father's house.

I was aware that Aunt Rose's words couldn't have made it plainer that I needed a husband, but I reassured myself that, if asked, I always had the power of refusal.

My explanation seemed to satisfy Mr. Lovejoy. He smiled, patted my hand (which was lying in my lap) and confided that he had recently purchased a lovely manor house in Kent, and his dream was to create a garden of such beauty that people would flock from all over to see it. He also confided that he had "looked over" the young women my aunt had invited during the course of the Season and he had not honored one of them with a proposal. They had struck him as frivolous, and none seemed deeply interested in gardening. I was different, however. I appreciated the beauty of a garden.

He next asked me about my daughter. I told him that Rosie was four and under the charge of her nurse. He nodded thoughtfully. "A girl in this situation is much better than a boy. It could work out."

The man was clearly thinking of making me an offer.

I could not marry Mr. Lovejoy and spend the rest of my life talking about gardens. I was trying to come up with a way to distract him when Mark came to my rescue. I had not known he was on the path behind me, but he and Lady Ann Morse came into view just then and I jumped to my feet to greet them.

Mark looked from me to little Mr. Lovejoy and lifted one blond eyebrow. I said, "How nice to see you Mr. Kingston. Miss Morse...." I bowed my head in acknowledgement of her superior status.

She gave me a strained smile. Mark said, "When Lady Ann suggested the gardens I thought I was going to see trees and flowers. But this is extraordinary."

"Isn't it?" I agreed. "Mr. Lovejoy is an expert on them, and I have been vastly entertained by his knowledge."

Mark's blue eyes were filled with amusement as they met mine. "How nice," he said.

I had not seen Mark with Lady Ann before. I had seen him with the girls whom Aunt Rose had picked for the earl, but Lady Ann had not been among that group. She was a little older—perhaps even twenty—and she wasn't particularly pretty. But her hazel eyes looked intelligent and when she spoke her voice was beautiful.

The four of us stood in conversation for a few minutes and then I said brightly that we had better carry on or we would be late for tea. Lady Ann agreed with me and the four of us moved off together to go back to the house.

*

Aunt Rose announced at tea that the evening's entertainment would be a dance in the drawing room. Almost everyone made noises of appreciation. I was quiet.

A dance, I thought with dread. Was I going to have to watch the earl dancing with the gorgeous Lady Mary Winstanley? Was I going to have to partner with Mr. Lovejoy and listen to more about gardens? Or Mr. Fenwick and listen to hunting stories?

Mr. John Emmott, the young man who had been fishing with the earl, would be acceptable. I had sat next to him at dinner last evening and he seemed very pleasant.

The last man on Aunt Rose's list, Lord Castlewood, the heir to the Duke of Bramley, had never acknowledged me, but I had caught him looking at me. Aunt Rose had told me he was a bit of a rake, and whenever I felt his eyes on me I turned away.

I would be more comfortable sitting on the sidelines and not dancing at all. Unless the earl should ask me.... I shook my head. *Idiot. He's not here to dance with his...his...whatever I am to him. He is here to find an appropriate wife so he can beget a son so that Horrible Harold will never be able to inherit the earldom.*

I wondered if I could plead illness and stay in my room all night.

Aunt Rose would probably come herself to drag me out.

I was going to have to go.

I thought for a moment, then called up all my resources and bravely said aloud, *"Damn!!!"*

*

90

May was far more excited than I was about the dance. She chose one of the beautiful gowns Aunt Rose had bought me and I agreed with her choice. It was cut rather simply out of a lovely gold sarsenet material and fell gracefully to the tips of the golden shoes that matched. I had never worn gold before but the color looked nice on me. May was bubbling as she closed the tiny buttons that ran from my waist up my back. I always did my hair myself and I wore it in a chignon at the back of my head. May begged me to let her try something different and, after looking at her eager face, I allowed it.

She plaited my hair, which is rather long, and arranged the plaits as a crown on the top of my head. This exposed my entire neck, which made a startling difference to my appearance. I have large eyes but now they looked enormous. My décolletage suddenly seemed more exposed, especially since I didn't have my mother's pearls to break up the expanse of flesh. I looked down at my breasts nervously. "Is this dress too revealing?" I asked May.

She laughed at me. "No. You look beautiful, my lady. Well, you always look beautiful, but now you look..." She searched for a word then found it, "*Regal.*"

She was so pleased, and I didn't want to spoil her pleasure, even though I knew my lack of jewelry was bound to be a source of comment. I said, "You are a genius with hair, May. You should be a full-time lady's maid."

Her blue eyes shone. "That is my dream, my lady. I would love to be a real lady's maid. Now, let me look through your jewelry and see if we can find something that will set off that beautiful dress.

I had sold virtually every piece of jewelry I could get money for, and what was left was fairly pitiful. May was looking doubtfully at the few things she had chosen when a knock sounded at the door. May opened it and a footman stood there holding an elegant blue box. "This is for Lady Aston," he said. "Lady Baldock would like her to wear them this evening."

May received the box, closed the door and brought it over to me. It contained a pearl necklace that was far lovelier than my mother's had been, with matching earrings. There were also two gold combs for my hair, which May set in expertly.

Oh, Aunt Rose, I thought. *I have been so unappreciative of what you are trying to do for me. I'm sorry. Thank you for these!*

May clasped the pearls around my neck and in my ears. I stared in the mirror, and I no longer looked like a goose girl dressed up like a princess. I looked like....

"You look like a princess, my lady!" May said.

I smiled at her. She was so excited, and I knew it was all pretend. No matter how I might look, I was no princess. I was a widow with a child and not enough money. No borrowed pearls could hide that.

"Thank you for helping me, May," I said.

"The men will be lining up to dance with you, my lady," she said confidently.

There is only one man I want to dance with, I thought sadly, and he will be dancing with someone else.

On that cheerful thought I opened my bedroom door and walked down the hall to the staircase.

Chapter Fifteen

The furniture in the drawing room had been pushed back against the walls or removed. The Persian rug had also been taken away and the floor polished. A small orchestra fitted nicely into a corner, and with the furniture gone and the room opened up, there was enough room for forty people plus a dance floor.

The first thing I did was look around for the earl. I didn't see him, but I did see Mark. I was making my way toward him when I was intercepted by Mr. Fenwick, the sportsman.

"You're looking lovely this evening, Lady Aston," he said. "Quite regal."

"Thank you. You are looking rather splendid yourself, Mr. Fenwick."

He looked pleased. "I was looking for you when the first dance started but I hope I may have this second one."

I smiled. "Of course."

At this point the floor began to fill for a cotillion and I let my partner take my hand and lead me out to the floor.

I like to dance, and once I got into the rhythm of it I began to enjoy myself. I danced with Mr. Fenwick, then with Mr. Lovejoy, then with Mark. I danced with Mr. Emmott, the only one of Aunt Rose's group I liked but who wasn't interested in me. I also danced with a few older men who were good dancers and rather fun. I kept hoping the earl might ask me to dance, but he didn't. He seemed to be occupied with Lady Margaret Fleetwood.

The evening was halfway over when Lord Castlewood, the heir to the Duke of Albany, asked me to dance. He had been placed next to me at dinner the previous evening and I hadn't liked him. He had a way of looking at me, as if I were a piece of merchandise, that made me uncomfortable. On the surface his conversation had been unobjectionable, but I would rather listen to Mr. Lovejoy talk about gardens or Mr. Fenwick about shooting grouse than have Lord Castlewood looking at me while he talked.

Of course I had to accept his invitation, and when the dance was over he suggested we step out into the garden for some fresh air. It was getting warm in the drawing room and I would very much enjoy getting outdoors, but not with Lord Castlewood. However, he was the heir to a duke and I didn't know how to reject him, so I agreed.

The moon was so bright in the sky that the patio lay clearly before me. Unfortunately we were the only ones there. I took a long breath and said brightly, "The cool air does feel good. The drawing room was getting rather stuffy."

He said, "I have been watching you ever since you arrived."

Well, I knew that. I replied, "Have you?"

"You outshine every one of those silly girls who want me to marry them."

That was a surprising remark. I looked up at him and was further surprised to find he seemed serious. "I don't like innocent little girls," he said. "I like women."

That comment frightened me. "You know nothing about me, my lord," I said.

"I know you were married to a baronet who gambled away all his money and killed himself."

This was brutal but, unfortunately, true.

I said firmly, "I believe we have been alone out here for long enough, my lord. I would like to go back inside."

He reached out and grabbed my wrist. He held it so tightly that he was hurting me. "In a minute," he said and began to pull me toward him.

I tried to pull away but his hold on my wrist tightened. I was beginning to feel frightened when a soft but oddly dangerous voice said, "Let her go, Castlewood."

It was the earl.

Lord Castlewood released my wrist. "I wasn't going to harm her, Chiltern. All I wanted was a kiss."

"The lady doesn't want to kiss you."

As soon as I was free I ran to stand next to the earl.

From the safety of his side I said, "I most certainly don't."

My voice was trembling. The threat of violence had brought back too many bad memories.

The earl said, "I suggest you go back inside, Castlewood. Now."

It was the voice of a man who had fought across the battlefields of Portugal, Spain and France. Lord Castlewood went. The earl and I were alone on the patio.

"Are you all right, Laura?"

To my great embarrassment I began to cry. Through my sobs I managed to say, "No, I'm not all right. I don't want to marry any of these men. I should never have come here."

He pulled me into his arms and I cried into his shoulder. I wished I never had to leave the safety of his arms.

"You can remain at Chiltern." His voice sounded different and his body had stiffened. I thought he wanted me to step away from him, but when I started to move he didn't let me go.

"I can't stay at Chiltern. Aunt Rose was right about that too. Your wife wouldn't like me being there."

I had stopped crying but he didn't drop his arms. He said in a tense voice, "It would be all right if *you* were my wife."

I was stunned. Could he mean....?

I swallowed and said in a trembling voice, "Are you saying you would marry me?"

He put his hands on my shoulders and held me away so he could look at me. "No," he said. "I am *asking* you to marry me."

His eyes were intent upon my face. I drew a long breath and said, "If I were your wife I would be the happiest woman in the world."

His nostrils flared a little and his eyes narrowed. I took a step away from him and said, "I don't want you to marry me because you're sorry for me. I would hate to live with that."

His black brows lifted in surprise. "*Sorry for you?* I'm not sorry for you Laura. I love you! I've loved you for months."

I was stunned. I searched his face and said in bewilderment, "But...why didn't you tell me? If you loved me why did you let Aunt Rose pick out possible wives for you? Was it because I'm not high-born enough?"

All the muscles in his face tightened. I had the feeling that it was difficult for him to keep looking at me. He said in a staccato like voice, "I didn't ask you because I didn't want to burden you with a cripple. You are perfect. I am not."

I stared up into the light gray eyes that were looking down at me with such anguish. "What do you mean, you're crippled? I don't understand."

"I have bad dreams. I wake up and I'm sweating and shaking and it takes me a while to calm down. I've seen so much death, Laura. I carry it around inside me all the time. Sometimes I wonder if it would have been better if I had been killed."

I reached up and put my hand across his mouth. "Don't say that! Never say that!"

"That's why I never asked you to marry me, never let you guess my feelings. I didn't want to burden you with a husband who is defective. Better some unknown girl who will do her duty, give me an heir, and then go on to lead her own life."

I was shocked by this revelation. I cupped his face with my hands. The moon showed his beautiful gray eyes darkened with pain. He turned his face, kissed one of my hands and said, "It was only when I saw the men Aunt Rose had picked for you, and saw how you didn't like any of them. I thought then that you might be happier at Chiltern, and I would try not to bother you too much."

I let my arms fall to my sides and took a deep breath. "I didn't like them because I love you, my lord." I smiled up at him. "I have loved you for a long time."

His face changed and he said in a husky voice, "My name is Robert." Then he bent his beautiful dark head and kissed me.

It was a gentle kiss, a reassuring kiss, and I relaxed and leaned into him.

"Will you take a chance on me, Laura?" he asked.

"I will if you're willing to take a chance on me."

He grinned, the boy's grin I so loved, and said, "Shall we go inside and tell Aunt Rose?"

I thought that Aunt Rose might not be as pleased as he thought. She had never once mentioned the idea of a marriage between us. But I couldn't resist that grin. I smiled back and said, "Why not?"

Hand in hand, the two of us went back into the drawing room.

*

Robert extracted Aunt Rose from the group she was talking to and maneuvered her out into the hallway.

"What is it, Robert?" she asked, looking at the two of us. Her face lit with a smile. "Are you going to tell me you are both engaged?"

"That is exactly what we are going to tell you," Robert said. "I am happy to inform you, Aunt Rose, that Laura has agreed to marry me."

Aunt Rose's face went blank. "You and Laura?" she said to Robert.

My heart dropped. Clearly she was not delighted.

"Yes," Robert replied. "Laura and I are getting married."

She looked at me for the first time. Then she looked back to Robert. "Is there something else I should know?"

Robert looked puzzled. "What do you mean?"

I understood perfectly. My face was burning with a mixture of anger and humiliation as I said, "His lordship has always behaved like a perfect gentleman toward me, Aunt Rose."

Robert finally understood. In a voice that would have frozen the equator he said, "I have the utmost respect for Laura, Aunt Rose. I have asked her to marry me because I love her."

It was Aunt Rose's turn to flush. "I beg your pardon, Robert." She turned to me. "And I beg your pardon as well, Laura. Of course, neither of you would have done anything disreputable."

Robert took my hand into his.

Aunt Rose regarded the two of us thoughtfully. "Good heavens. I don't know why I didn't think of this match myself. You will suit each other admirably."

"We think so," Robert said evenly.

Aunt Rose's bosom inflated, the way it always did when she had an idea. "We shall all three of us return to the drawing room and I will make an announcement."

"We don't want an announcement, Aunt Rose," Robert replied immediately.

Thank you, I thought.

Aunt Rose was shaking her head. "Listen to me, Robert. Laura has been living unchaperoned at Chiltern ever since your return from France. There will be talk that she is in the family way, that you had to marry her. If I make the announcement now, and my husband and I show that we are pleased, it will go a long way toward suppressing unsavory rumors."

Robert sounded impatient as he replied, "We don't care what these people think, Aunt Rose. If their minds are in the gutter that is their problem, not ours."

Aunt Rose's bosom swelled another inch. "Robert, it is clear to everyone at this party that I have been trying to find Laura a husband. It is also clear that I am trying to find you a wife. This...news...happy though it has made me...*will* start rumors. It is important that we do all we can to protect Laura from such talk."

I looked at Aunt Rose with admiration. She had said the one thing that would infallibly make Robert agree with her. He proved me right by capitulating, "All right, but *I* will make the announcement."

Aunt Rose agreed. One didn't argue with Robert when he used that tone of voice.

The three of us waited until the music quieted between dances. Then we went inside. Robert stood at the front of the room facing the emptying dance floor and Aunt Rose and I stood off to the side. Robert didn't say a word but within seconds everyone in the room had turned to look at him.

How did he do that? I wondered.

He spoke in a quiet level voice that reached the farthest corners of the crowded room. "I have happy news to share with you this evening. Lady Laura Aston has agreed to be my wife."

There was movement among the crowd as people looked at each other in surprise. But quiet still reigned as Robert remained in place.

"As most of you probably noticed, my dear Aunt Rose invited me to this lovely house party hoping I would find a spouse. It was when I saw Lady Aston with other men admiring her that I realized I didn't want her to marry someone else, I wanted her to marry me." I tore my eyes away from him for a second to look around the room. All eyes were glued to Robert. He was saying, "She has done me the honor of reciprocating my regard and accepting my proposal. I am the happiest of men and I know my wonderful aunt will break out the champagne in honor of our betrothal."

He turned, reached out his hand to me and smiled. My heart melted. That smile. I would do anything he wanted when he smiled at me that way. I gave him my hand and we began to tour the room, accepting best wishes from all the guests. The promised champagne arrived. Everyone drank. Everyone danced some more. I had so much champagne that I felt a little wobbly. Robert kindly took my arm and escorted me up the stairs to my room. He kissed me lightly at the door and said good night.

When I gave birth to Rosie I had thought it was the happiest day of my life. This day was also the happiest day of my life. I would treasure the memory of both occasions forever in my heart.

It was when I got into bed that I realized Mark had not been in the room when Robert made the announcement of our coming

nuptials. How happy he will be for me, I thought. I looked forward
to seeing him tomorrow.

Chapter Sixteen

I woke later than usual the following morning and lay in bed hugging to myself the knowledge that I was going to marry Robert. I wouldn't have to leave Chiltern. I wouldn't have to disrupt Rosie's life by dragging her away from the place she thought of as home. I would never have to worry about money again. But over and above all of these wonderful things, I was going to marry the man I loved.

I sprang out of bed and rang the bell that went to the servant's quarters. *Wait until May hears my news*, I thought. I would make her my official lady's maid and she would never have to dust furniture or beat rugs again.

She appeared quickly and her pretty face was beaming. "I heard the news, my lady! I am so happy for you! Everyone at Chiltern will be so happy! You are a good mistress! We all love you! Oh, I am so happy!"

I held out my arms and she came to give me a big hug.

"I'm happy too," I said when we separated. "I hated the thought of leaving Chiltern. His lordship has saved me a great deal of worry."

She cocked her head and looked at me, amusement clear in her blue eyes. "He's in love with you, my lady. We all saw it."

I stared at her in astonishment. "You saw that he loved me?"

"It was obvious, my lady. The way he would look at you. The way his eyes always followed you whenever you were in a room."

I couldn't believe I was hearing this. The servants knew that Robert was in love with me and I had been oblivious. How had that happened?

May went to the wardrobe and selected a dress. "I don't think Mr. Kingston will be happy though."

"What do you mean by that? I think he will be very happy for me. Why shouldn't he be?"

"Because he is also in love with you, my lady."

She had thrown me so off balance that I felt as if the floor beneath me was rocking. "You are mistaken, May," I said in a voice I tried to make firm. "You are seeing things that do not exist."

She laid the dress out on the bed. "How could he not love you? My lady, not only are you beautiful, you are kind. When you look at one of our footmen you don't see a 'footman.' You see a person. You notice if one of us is not feeling well. You praise us when we do something well. We all love you because you care about us."

I didn't know what to say to her. "My father was a vicar," I finally managed. "He cared for every person in his flock. I learned from him."

I looked at the dress laid out on the bed and said, "I think it's time to get dressed."

"Yes, my lady."

She helped me into the dress and did up all the back buttons. Then I went to the mirror to do my hair. I looked at myself as if I was looking at a stranger. I knew I was pretty, but my father had discouraged any pride I might take in my looks. My face had been given to me by God, he said, and I had no cause to take pride in it. The outside of me didn't matter. God was only interested in what was inside.

Since this comment was so obviously the truth, I had never tried to call attention to my looks. I had worn my hair parted in the middle and pulled into the same chignon at the nape of my neck since I was sixteen. I never wore any kind of cosmetic. I...

May had come up behind me and now we both looked at my image in the mirror. "You look like a painting of the Madonna, my lady. So beautiful, so serene, so good. The rest of the staff will be so happy you are to stay with us."

Again, I didn't know how to reply. All I could do was look at her helplessly and say, "Will you help me do my hair?"

"Of course, my lady. I have always wanted to do a little more with your hair."

"No!" I could not go downstairs with a new hairdo just now.

She smiled at me the way a mother would smile at a nervous child. "I will do it the same as always."

When I left my room to go downstairs to breakfast all of my earlier happiness had turned into worry. What if May was right? What if Mark wasn't happy for me? What if he did love me? I was a bundle of nerves by the time I reached the breakfast room. I inhaled deeply twice, stretched my shoulders, and went into the room.

*

Very few men were in the room, as most of them had gone out shooting. Mark didn't shoot but he wasn't in the room. I didn't know if I should be relieved about that or not. If we met here he would have to put up a good front about my betrothal, which would be easier for me than if we met privately. But Mark was my friend. For a long time he had been my only friend. I loved him, but as a friend. I devoutly hoped that May was wrong about his feelings for me. Either way, it would be fairer to him if we met when he could speak to me honestly.

Lady Mary Winstanley was at the table as was Lady Margaret Fleetwood. Lady Mary's beautiful face was rigid with dislike as I took a seat a few places down from her on the opposite side of the table. "You have pulled off a veritable coup, Lady Aston," she said in a voice so cold I could feel the icicles. "Lord Chiltern is the catch of the Season."

"He is a very fine man," I replied in a steady voice.

The other women at the table were looking at me speculatively and suddenly I was angry. Who were these people to judge me? To judge Robert? I stood up, looked up and down the table and said, "You don't have to bother counting the months. I am not with child. Lord Chiltern has always respected me. He is an honorable man, and I am happy he asked me to be his wife."

With that I turned and stalked out of the room, stopping only once at the table where the breakfast was laid out to pick up two scones. I was hungry.

*

May brought me coffee from the kitchen and I drank it with my two scones. I was wiping my mouth when a knock sounded on my door. I nodded at May and she went to open it.

It was Robert and I thought he looked happy too. He was dressed for riding and I said brilliantly, "Are you going for a ride?"

"We are," he returned. "It's the only way I can get you alone."

I said, "I'll be downstairs in ten minutes."

He lifted a perfect black eyebrow. "You propose to change your clothes in ten minutes?"

His skeptical voice reinforced the lifted eyebrow. I looked at May and she bit her lip. "Fifteen minutes?" she said doubtfully.

"Fifteen it is," Robert said with a grin.

My heart swelled with love. I smiled back and said, "Go."

He laughed then turned and went out the door. I watched his back until he disappeared.

May said, "Turn around, my lady and let me get you out of that dress.

I made it downstairs in sixteen minutes. Robert, who had been looking at his watch, said he would give me the extra minute as a gift. He was a generous winner.

*

We walked down to the stable together and I told Robert about my encounter with the people at the breakfast table this morning. "I hope Aunt Rose won't be horrified when she hears how blunt I was."

"She was afraid they would think the worst and you have put that rumor to rest. How can she object?"

"That is exactly what I will say if she tries to scold me."

"Tell her I'm proud of you for standing up to them."

I peeked up at him from under the brim of my hat. "Are you proud of me?"

"I am so proud of you that I feel like shouting from the rooftops, "Laura Aston is going to marry me!!!"

I could face anybody knowing he felt like that about me.

*

Aunt Rose had some lovely horses in her stable. I rode a very pretty gray and Robert rode a very large bay. We took a path he thought would be unknown to the rest of the guests and we had a wonderful ride in the morning sunshine. I didn't think I had ever been this happy in my life. Even when Rosie was born, and I held her in my arms for the first time, my happiness had been tarnished by the fear I felt for her with Tom having so much power over our lives.

We dismounted on the banks of one of the streams that ran through the estate and Robert took his coat off for me to sit on. I was going to object that it would get dirty, but he had made such a grand display of fanning it out and setting it down that I kept my mouth closed and sat.

"All I can see of you is your hat," he complained when he joined me.

I promptly took it off. He circled my face with his hands, bent his head and kissed me. Tom had rarely bothered to kiss me, being too occupied with more fundamental matters, and the feel of a man's lips on mine was new.

I kissed him back, loving the feeling of his strength against me, the feel of his shirt under my fingers, the smell of his skin. He deepened the gentle kiss into something more demanding and I liked it. I kissed him and kissed him until finally he put his hands on my shoulders and put me away from him.

I looked up, blinking in surprise at the abrupt separation.

His voice was dark and husky as he said, "I want to get married soon, Laura. I don't want to wait."

I didn't want to wait either, but... "What about the ladies who will be counting months?"

"Do you really care about them?"

105

"Not at all."

He lifted my hand and cradled it against his cheek. "I love you so much," he said. And raised my hand to his mouth. The touch of his lips on my hand was almost as thrilling as his kiss. It felt like a seal of commitment. A promise that he would always be there for me, that I would never be alone again.

"Let's decamp from this party tomorrow morning," he said. "I want you to myself."

I agreed to this proposition with all my heart.

We rode back to the house together and sought out Aunt Rose. Robert told her we would be leaving early the following morning. She looked at us and tears ran down her cheeks.

"I am so happy for you both. I still cannot believe how blind I was."

"It was my fault," Robert said. "I should have told Laura how I felt sooner. It's just…I was afraid I would be putting her in an awkward position. She would think she had to marry me if she wanted to stay at Chiltern and I didn't want her to feel that way. I wanted her to feel free to say yes or no, and coming to this house party did just that. You were right when you said she had to marry, Aunt Rose, and when I saw the collection of candidates you had collected, I knew Laura would be happier with me."

"*Much happier*," I said, smiling up at him.

"You must let me help plan your wedding," Aunt Rose said next.

"Laura doesn't want a big wedding," Robert replied immediately.

I didn't, of course, but he hadn't yet consulted me on the matter.

Aunt Rose's bosom swelled. "You are the earl, Robert. You owe it to your tenants and your neighbors to have a magnificent wedding that all of them can attend."

I looked at her and thought, Aunt Rose has never had a daughter whose wedding she could plan. And she has been so good to me. If it weren't for her I would never have met Robert.

"Nonsense," I said looking at Robert meaningfully. "Of course I want a big wedding. And of course I want Aunt Rose to plan the whole affair. I'll help her where I can."

Robert looked stunned. I knew how much he was looking forward to a quiet life, but….

I raised my brows at him and nodded at Aunt Rose, who had done so much for both of us over the years. Then I turned back to her, put my arms around her and said, "You have always been my second mother."

I couldn't see Aunt Rose's face, but Robert could. I heard him say resignedly. "All right. We'll have the wedding of the year Aunt Rose. But only if you leave me out of it."

I stepped back from her so I could see her face. It was radiant. She looked ten years younger. "Men are useless at planning grand events," she told Robert. "All you will need to do is present yourself at the church at the proper time."

"I think I can do that," he said.

We left her in the rose garden and went into the house. "How are we going to get home tomorrow?" I asked.

"Laura, I have moved thousands of troops on shorter notice. I guarantee I will be able to arrange for us to leave tomorrow morning."

I laughed up at him. "Yes, sir!"

He bent and kissed me lightly on the lips.

Chapter Seventeen

I looked for Mark several times during the course of the afternoon, but he never appeared. After dinner, Lord Sommers, who was a force in the Whig party, invited Robert and me to play whist with him and his wife. I hadn't played cards outside of children's games for ages, but I had used to play with my father and was a decent player. Robert, I soon discovered, was an excellent card player. The Sommers' were gracious losers and when I went upstairs to my room I was pleased with the evening and looking forward to going home tomorrow.

I opened the door expecting to find May waiting for me, but it was Mark who was standing in front of my window, his eyes on the door.

My heart jumped. "Mark! You frightened me! What are you doing here? I've been looking for you all day. You weren't in the room when Robert announced our marriage plans last night and I wanted to tell you myself."

He didn't move away from the window, just stood there looking at me. "I heard it from Morrow," he said in an expressionless voice.

Lord Morrow was one of the leaders of the Tory party. I had noticed Mark in his company a few times during the course of the week. Robert had also been talking to political men, but his preferred party was the Whigs.

The moon was shining in the window and its light fell on Mark's hair, making it gleam like purest gold. I walked forward until I was close enough to see his face clearly. His blue eyes were darker than usual, and they bore an expression I had never seen in them before. It took a moment for me to realize he was angry. Instinctively I took a step back. I cast a quick look at my dressing room door and wondered if May was there.

Mark said, "It came as quite a shock. You always told me you would never marry again. I suppose you found it impossible to turn down an earl."

I rushed to justify myself. "I was taken by complete surprise, Mark. I hadn't a clue that the earl was going to propose."

I almost said that I loved Robert, the words were on the tip of my tongue. Then instinct said perhaps it would be better not to go down that particular path. I said instead, "Just think, Mark. This means Rosie and I can remain at Chiltern forever. I won't have to move in with my father and his horrible wife. I won't have to become a governess or a school mistress. We can stay right where we are. This is such a blessing for us."

In a deeply bitter voice he said, "*I* love you, Laura. I have loved you for a long time. And now, when finally I have the funds to support us in a comfortable fashion, you are going to marry someone else. An earl! There is no way I can compete with that."

So May had been right after all. I said gently, "I had no idea you loved me, Mark. You never said anything. You have been my friend ever since I came to Chiltern. I would never want to hurt you."

A muscle twitched along his jaw and his hands clenched. The air was suddenly tense with suppressed violence, and I looked toward my dressing room again, hoping May would appear.

Mark's voice shook as he said, "I have recently purchased a manor house in Somerset for us to live in. You are so beautiful, Laura, so clearly a lady. You outshine all these silly girls here at Lady Baldock's. With you at my side I could be elected to Parliament. I could be an important man, someone whom people would look up to."

He had said he loved me, but he wanted to marry me because he thought I would help him become an "important man." My sympathy for him began to wane. I said, "Your aunt must have left you a great deal of money, Mark, if you can afford to buy a manor house."

His eyes narrowed and a white line appeared around his mouth. "I am not a Midas, like the earl, but I inherited enough money to live comfortably. For *us* to live comfortably."

Where had the Mark I knew gone?

Don't be an idiot, I told myself. He's just upset because I am marrying someone else. I wet my lips with my tongue and said, "If you have bought a house, I assume you will be leaving your post at Chiltern."

"Of course I will be leaving. I never meant that position to be something permanent. It was just something to do until my great aunt died."

I stared at him, at the flawless face, the golden hair, the broad shoulders. Had this magnificent exterior been hiding a stranger? A man I didn't recognize at all? I said, "Perhaps one of the girls you met here at Baldock Hall..."

I broke off as he made a gesture of dismissal. "I didn't come to Baldock Hall to meet women. I went to meet their husbands and their fathers—the men who sit in Parliament and rule the country. The men I will need to help my career when I get elected to Parliament."

"Ah." It was the best I could manage.

"I shall have to find someone else to marry now, but there will never be another like you, Laura." He looked at me and I had to fight to remain in place. He was scaring me. "You attract people," he said. "They like you. And you know how to run the house of an important man."

He had said nothing more about love.

As I stared at him, at this man who had been my best friend, a shiver ran up and down my spine. If Robert hadn't intervened, and if Mark had asked me to marry him, I might have accepted. I couldn't bear to stay at Chiltern if Robert had married another woman, and I hadn't saved enough money to start a school. I would have trusted Mark, my dear friend. Another shiver ran through me at the thought.

My dressing room door opened and May's blonde head appeared around it. "Do you need me, my lady?"

I could have kissed her. "Yes, May, you can help me get ready for bed. Mr. Kingston is just leaving."

*

Mark didn't join Robert and me in the carriage the following morning. Robert told me that Mark had decided to remain until the house party officially ended, that Aunt Rose had said she would make certain he had transport back to Chiltern.

I had lain awake a long time last night thinking about our conversation, and had come to the conclusion that I had overreacted. Mark had every reason to think his suit would be acceptable to me. A closeness had developed between us during the time we were alone together at Chiltern Hall and, while I had thought of him as a friend, he had been thinking of me as something more.

I was partly to blame for Mark's reaction to the news of my marriage. He had been hurt and his hurt had taken the form of anger. I decided not to say anything to Robert about our encounter. Mark was leaving Chiltern and that would put an end to any relationship between us.

So it was just Robert and I in the carriage and we sat close together and told each other all sorts of things about our lives. It was pure bliss to have him all to myself, and I think he felt the same way about me.

Chapter Eighteen

When we arrived home Robert called the servants together and told them about our upcoming marriage. Every single face broke into a smile as they heard the news. When Robert finished, Mason stepped forward. "I know I am speaking for all the staff when I say you have made us very happy, my lord. We have come to know Lady Aston during her tenure here and we all respect and admire her." He paused and looked from Robert to me. Absurdly, I felt tears spring to my eyes. Mason smiled at me and said, "We are delighted to hear such good news."

Tears began to run down my cheeks and Robert passed me a handkerchief. I managed to say, "Thank you, Mason. Thank you everyone." I wiped my cheeks and said in a trembling voice, "I am very happy."

"Then why are you crying?" It was Robert and his voice was gently teasing.

"I don't know," I replied and mopped some new tears.

Robert thanked the servants for their dedication to me and to Chiltern. He ended by saying, "Now I think it is time for you to get back to your various jobs."

*

Telling our news to the girls was a little more complicated. I knew Rosie would be happy; she liked Robert very much. And Margaret was very attached to me. I wasn't certain about Elizabeth, however. She had a mind of her own, that child, and little hesitation about showing how she felt.

Next Robert and I gathered the children around the big table in the nursery playroom. Rosie sat in the middle between Margaret and Elizabeth. "I have called you together for a happy announcement," Robert began.

Three pairs of eyes, two blue and one brown, stared at him.

He glanced at me then said, "I have asked Lady Laura to marry me and she has accepted."

Stunned silence from the girls.

Robert added, "I hope this news will make you as happy as it has made me."

Margaret spoke first, addressing Robert. "Does this mean that Lady Laura will be our aunt?"

Before Robert could answer Rosie asked, "Does this mean you will be my Papa?"

"Would you like me to be your Papa, Rosie?" he asked gently.

"Oh yes! My Papa is dead and I would love you to be my new one!"

She gave Robert a big smile filled with white baby teeth. and he smiled back. "I will be happy to be your Papa, Rosie." Turning to his eldest niece, he asked, "What do you think, Margaret?"

She glanced at Rosie, said, "Our Papa is dead too," and turned back to the two of us.

Robert didn't reply so I asked, "Would you like Uncle Robert to be your Papa too, Margaret?"

"Yes." She looked at him hopefully.

Robert blinked twice, then said, "It would make me very happy if you would call me *Papa*, Margaret."

Rosie, who adored Margaret, said generously, "You can share my Mama if you want to."

"Can I?" Margaret asked, looking at me eagerly.

I said, "It would make me very happy if you wanted to call me *Mama*, Margaret."

Margaret's smile was almost as big as Rosie's had been.

Robert and I next turned to Elizabeth, who had been quiet thus far. "What do you think about this, Elizabeth?" I asked.

She looked at me, a line between her brows. "Does this mean you won't be our governess anymore?"

I knew how much Elizabeth disliked change and said as gently as I could, "I am afraid we will have to get you another governess.

But I will still see you every day and we can still do things together."

Her troubled blue eyes went from me to Robert then back to me. "You're not really our Mama and Papa," she said. "Our real Mama and Papa are dead."

Rosie said urgently, "We need a papa, Elizabeth. A papa is better than an uncle."

I ignored Rosie and said to Elizabeth, "You are right, Elizabeth. Sadly, your mother and father are dead. But you are a little girl—you are all little girls—and little girls need a mother and a father. Little girls need to know that their future is secure, that they will always be protected and loved. And the best way to accomplish these goals is for little girls to have a mama and a papa."

Elizabeth nodded slowly. "Do I have to call you Mama?" she asked.

"You can call me by whatever name makes you comfortable," I said gently. "If you want to continue calling me *Lady Laura* that will be perfectly fine."

Elizabeth looked at Margaret, who sat on the other side of Rosie. "Are you going to call them *Mama* and *Papa*?"

"Yes!"

She looked back at us. "Well....I suppose it will be all right."

I went over to the table and bent to place a kiss on Elizabeth's soft curls. "I am honored," I said.

Elizabeth produced a faint smile.

Robert and I looked at each other in relief.

Chapter Nineteen

Our wedding was scheduled for October 14, just four weeks after Robert's announcement at Aunt Rose's house party. She was insistent that we wait at least a month because "otherwise people will talk." Robert wanted to get married immediately, but I listened to Aunt Rose. I wanted Robert's reputation to remain as spotless as I knew it to be.

Aunt Rose was indefatigable. She planned a grand reception for the wedding party and our other guests, to be held in the drawing room and dining room. She also planned celebrations for all of Chiltern's tenants and the local villagers to be held on the vast lawns surrounding the house. A giant tent was erected on the front lawn from which food could be served to the lesser folk. I will not go into how Aunt Rose decided who among the locals deserved to be invited into the house and who to relegate to the lawn. Suffice it to say it was a delicate situation. If I had my choice, I would have had the whole affair out on the lawns. If I *really* had my choice, I would have had a small wedding breakfast for just the immediate family. But, of course, Aunt Rose was not interested in my opinion.

Robert and I had driven out to visit my father shortly after we returned from the house party. His dreadful wife, Violet, was so awed by the presence of an earl in her house that she scarcely said a word. I could see that Papa was impressed by Robert, and not because of his title. Papa was very good at seeing into people's hearts (with the exception of the horrid Violet), and what he saw in Robert must have pleased him very much. As we were leaving he said to me, "You have found a good man this time, Laura. I had so many doubts the last time you married, but this time I am thoroughly happy."

I threw my arms around his neck and hugged him.

He said in my ear, "I am so sorry to have driven you away, my dearest daughter. If I had known that would happen I would never have…"

I leaned back and put a finger across his lips to stop him talking. His familiar hazel eyes were sad. I said, "There's nothing further to be said, Papa. There is nothing I would change. Tom was not a good husband, but he gave me Rosie. And Robert...well, he is just the best man in the world. I am so happy I sometimes feel as if I will float off the ground!"

He gave me the luminous smile that everyone who knew him loved. "God bless you, my daughter. And thank you. Thank you for asking me to marry you to this fine young man."

*

It had rained on the day I married Tom, but on the day I married Robert the sun shone brightly. It shone on the vast expanse of clipped green lawn that was covered with tables swathed in white linen. The food and drink were bountiful. While the lesser folk had their food outdoors, the upper class congregated in the house to drink champagne and eat a sumptuous meal. Champagne flowed both outside and inside. The food was outstanding. Everyone congratulated us.

The reception was lovely, but the significant part of the day for Robert and me had occurred when we stood in front of Papa in the village church and made our promises to each other. My whole heart was in my eyes when I looked up at Robert's grave face and promised to have him for better for worse, for richer for poorer, in sickness and in health, to love, cherish and obey until death did us part. When he put the ring on my finger he lifted my hand to his lips and kissed it.

My only thought had been, *Thank you, God. Thank you for giving me this wonderful man.*

After we returned to the house, Robert and I spent an hour outdoors greeting all our lesser guests and well-wishers, and then we went inside and did the same with our noble company.

"My face hurts from smiling," I confided to Robert as I drank my third glass of champagne.

"I'm ready to leave if you are," he said.

We were having a short wedding trip. Robert knew of a small hotel on the coast near Hythe and he had reserved an apartment for us. We were only going for a week. I didn't want to leave the children for too long and Robert had a few projects he was anxious about.

We took the phaeton. May and MacAlister had left right after the wedding with our bags so it was just the two of us driving along the coast on a beautiful late autumn afternoon. We talked about the wedding first, then I asked Robert about MacAlister. Before he arrived I hadn't known that army officers had a soldier assigned to them to act as their personal servant, and I was curious about him. I knew that he and Robert were very close.

Robert told me that MacAlister came from the Highlands, from the area around Kintyre. He had become a soldier for the same reason so many other young men joined the British army. There was nothing for him at home and the army would pay him a salary.

"When I was wounded at Salamanca he took care of me like a mother," Robert said. "I couldn't leave him behind after Waterloo; he would have been discharged from the army with no prospects and little money. London will be teeming with dismissed soldiers looking to make a living and there was no way for him to earn money back in Kintyre. So I asked him to be my valet. It has worked out very well. He's a good friend."

"How nice. I don't have any history with May, but I like her and we chatter away like two old chums," I had replied.

We were an hour from Hythe when one of the horses suddenly went lame. Robert cursed under his breath and handed me the reins. "Let me take a look," he said and swung down from the carriage. It was growing dark and we were alone on the road.

Robert came back to the phaeton and reported grimly, "The whole shoe came off. I can't imagine why Walsh sent us off if the shoe was loose."

"You can't get it back on temporarily?"

"It's gone, Laura. If I find it I can probably get it back on. I have extra nails and a hammer in the back of the phaeton. But I need the shoe. Timothy's feet are difficult. The blacksmith always makes a barred shoe for him."

I said, "It can't be very far away. I'll help you look."

"No," he said. "I need you to hold the horses. I'll look."

Last night the moon had lighted up the landscape when I looked out the window. Not tonight. *Where are you, when we need you?* I thought with annoyance as I scanned the cloudy sky.

I waited for almost an hour. In all that time I was passed by three carriages and one rider, none of whom was carrying a horseshoe that would fit Timothy.

"I've got it!" Robert came up to the side of the phaeton and smiled up at me. His white teeth gleamed in the dark. "Can you get me the bag of tools I have in the back of the phaeton? They're in a leather sack. I'll hold the horses while you look."

I crawled into the back of the phaeton, felt around and finally touched leather. I picked it up, climbed back to the front seat and climbed down from the phaeton. I brought the sack to Robert and, as I was handing it to him, the moon came out.

"About time," Robert said as he took the bag from me. We both looked up. The moon seems to have moved into an area of clear sky," he said, "The light should hold long enough for me to get this shoe on." I took Timothy's rein. Robert opened his tool sack and went to work.

I spoke soothingly to Timothy, who twitched his ears but didn't move. His partner, Gordon, was getting restless from standing on the road for so long and I reached over to pet his muzzle and talk to him as well. The two chestnut geldings made a beautiful pair, certain to catch the eye of anyone who beheld them.

I could clearly hear the sound of the nails being pounded into Timothy's foot. The horse, bless him, stood like a rock. Finally I heard Robert say, "It's on." He sounded grim. "Not the neatest job in the world but it should hold until we get to Hythe."

I walked the two horses forward and Robert watched Timothy. "He seems all right," I said.

Robert nodded. "He's not limping. Let's get back into the carriage and carry on."

He lifted me into the phaeton, went around the horses to the other side and climbed up himself. I gave him the reins and he said, "I'm sorry, Laura. This is a hell of a way to start a wedding trip."

I laid my head on his shoulder for a moment. "I don't mind. And I'm very impressed that you have the talents of a farrier."

He said matter-of-factly, "When your life depends upon the reliability of your horse you learn some basic skills."

He lifted his hands and we moved forward again.

*

The moon came in and out as we finished the drive. It had taken two hours, as Robert didn't trust the shoe at a trot. We were both starving by the time we reached the Mermaid Inn. One of Chiltern's grooms had come with May and MacAlister and he was there to take charge of the horses. The hotel's groom assured us that he would get a blacksmith to put Timothy's shoe back on correctly.

Robert lifted me down from the phaeton and the feel of his strong hands around my waist made me shiver. We went indoors and the innkeeper, a freckled, big-shouldered man, showed us up the stairs to our rooms. Robert opened the door to the first place we would inhabit as man and wife.

We walked into a charming sitting room with a big window that I thought must look out on the Channel. We stood together in the middle of the room and Robert put his arm around my shoulder. I rested my head against his shoulder.

"I finally have you to myself," he said and bent his head to kiss my hair.

A door opened behind us and MacAlister's voice said, "I see you have arrived my lord, my lady."

Robert's arm dropped and we turned around. May was standing next to MacAlister smiling at us.

"It took ye awhile," MacAlister said in his distinctive Scottish accent.

"We're late because Timothy lost a shoe," Robert returned. "How long have you been here?"

"We were here by five."

"Have you eaten?" I asked.

MacAlister replied, "That we have, my lady. They fed us fine in the kitchen."

May said, "I laid out your dinner gown, my lady. The kitchen is holding food for you."

"Thank God. We're starving," Robert said.

"If you will take me to my bedroom, May, I will dress as quickly as I can."

"It's this way, my lady," she responded, gesturing to the door.

A hallway led off the sitting room and I followed May as she led me out. We passed two doors and she opened the third. "This is your dressing room, my lady."

I had never had a dressing room before, although I would have one when we returned home. The lord's bedroom at Chiltern was huge, with doors on opposite walls leading into one dressing room for the earl and one for the countess. I had seen it when Aunt Rose gave me a tour of the house when I first arrived.

A very pretty evening gown in pale cream satin was laid out on the bed. It was my favorite of all the gowns Aunt Rose had bought me in London and I had told May I wanted to wear it on our first night in Hythe.

May helped me disrobe and then she guided the beautiful dress over my head. As I was standing in front of a tall pier glass mirror and as she was buttoning up the back, I contemplated myself.

The gown brought out the creamy color of my skin, which is why I liked it so much. It flattered me. In this gown, I thought I looked almost beautiful.

I sat at the dressing table and May unknotted my chignon and brushed out my hair. "What if I arranged it on top of your head, my lady? That style would show off your neck. You have a beautiful neck, my lady, and your chignon hides it."

I wanted very much to be beautiful for Robert tonight, so I said recklessly, "Go ahead."

When May finished the new hairdo I stood up and faced her. "Oh my lady," she breathed. "You look...you look like a...queen."

I crossed to the pier glass and looked in. My eyes widened. I did look beautiful. I said to May, "I think I'm always going to wear this color."

"You can wear any color and be beautiful, my lady," she replied.

But I knew that this color, this dress, these beautiful pearls—a wedding gift from Robert that May had clasped around my neck—were something special. I never wore makeup but my cheeks were pink and my eyes were bright. I was married to the man I loved. I had never been this happy in my entire life, and I looked it.

Chapter Twenty

When Robert made the inn reservation, he had been informed that there was a previous reservation for the same week. This had been a disappointment. He wanted us to have the place to ourselves and had immediately booked the three remaining suites to keep them unoccupied. The other (unwanted) residents were before us when we came into the dining room, but the management had put them at a table farthest from the window table, where we were to sit.

I was feeling nervous. My experience of marital sex had been brutal, and while I knew Robert would never want to hurt me, the marriage act was the marriage act. To be truthful, it had always felt as if I was being split apart. It hurt and it made me bleed. However, I was determined not to let Robert see my fear. I understood that sex was important to men. I understood that they enjoyed it. I wanted him to think I welcomed him.

"Would you care for some wine, my lord?" the waiter asked.

"Yes. A bottle of champagne, please."

While they were speaking, my eyes touched on the other couple. Their heads had whipped around at the words "my lord," and I caught them staring at us. I looked back at Robert, hoping they weren't the sort of people who liked to socialize with their fellow visitors. I wanted to have Robert all to myself before we had to go home to the children and the house.

We had an excellent dinner, which I couldn't do justice to. When Robert asked if I was feeling all right, I told him I had eaten so much at the reception that I wasn't hungry. We chatted about the wedding and Timothy's shoe and then it was time to go upstairs.

May was waiting to help me out of my dinner gown and into my night dress. I tried to be matter of fact, but she kept looking at me with bright happy eyes and brilliant smiles. I sat at the dressing table while she undid my hair and brushed it out. When unbound it was long, falling halfway down my back; brushing it required a lot of effort. When she was finished I stood and told her she could seek her own bed, that I would see her in the morning.

"Yes, my lady." She sighed. "You look so beautiful."

I took a quick glance at my figure in the mirror. Having Rosie had initially loosened my belly, but all the gardening I did at Aston Hall had tightened it up. I tied the sash on my satin robe (another gift from Aunt Rose) and went into the bedroom.

Robert was before me. He had opened the window curtains and was standing there looking out. He wore a black silk dressing gown, and he turned when he heard the door open. He held out his hand and I went to join him.

The moon was shining brightly in the sky, illuminating the waters of the Channel that lay beyond the inn's lawn. I leaned my cheek against Robert's arm and said, "How beautiful."

He looked down at me. The moon's light fell on his ebony hair and played off the planes of his face. His long lashes cast a shadow on his moonlit cheek. "I love you," I said softly.

Please God I can make him happy, I prayed.

He untied the belt of my robe and pushed it off my shoulders. It fell to the ground in a heap. He touched the swell of my breast with one gentle finger, then bent down, put his arms under my knees and lifted me into his arms as if I weighed nothing. I put my arms around his neck as he carried me to the bed. He discarded his own robe and followed me, turning me to face him as his naked body stretched out next to mine. Then he kissed me.

It was so sweet, that kiss, and I responded. He cupped my face between his hands, as if I were a flower, and continued kissing me. His lips felt warm and comforting against mine. When the tip of his tongue slid gently into my mouth I was surprised. Tom had never done anything like this. Tentatively I touched his tongue with my own. Gradually the kiss deepened, and I felt myself respond.

His mouth left mine to trail a line of gentle kisses down my neck, right to the top of my night dress. He pushed the silk material out of his way and moved his lips, gently and caressingly, to my bared breast. As he took my nipple between his lips and began to play with it with it I felt a wave of sensation ripple through the lower part of my body. I closed my eyes and felt his hand slowly caressing my waist, my hips, my thighs. A tension I had never known began to build between my legs. Then he started to push up my night dress.

I stiffened. I couldn't help it. He looked up at me and said, "Is anything wrong, Laura?"

"N...no." Then I said the thing I had sworn never to say, "It's just that Tom always hurt me."

An expression I had never seen before flashed in his eyes, then was gone. He said softly, "If I hurt you, tell me and I'll stop."

I looked up into his gray eyes. This was Robert, I told myself. I could trust him.

The fear that had come so suddenly began to recede. I reached up to run my fingers through his thick black hair. He touched me and caressed me and all the time the tense sensation kept building and building. My legs parted as if on their own volition and when he came into me it didn't hurt. I found myself opening my legs wider to make it easier for him to come deeper. All of my attention was now focused on the tension his movements were building. My breath came faster and faster. Then, when I thought I could bear it no longer, the tension exploded and waves of a powerful physical sensation rocked my body. I heard Robert cry out. When it was over and we were holding each other tightly, Robert kept saying my name over and over, as if it were a prayer. Then he lifted himself away from me, supporting himself by his arms so he wouldn't crush me. He looked down into my face and said softly, "Are you all right?"

"Yes." I smiled up at him. "I am more than all right. I am..." I searched for a word to express what he had done for me. "*Wonderful*," was the best I could come up with.

He smiled back. "It was indeed wonderful. Thank you, my love, for agreeing to become my wife."

He lowered himself to the bed beside me and I snuggled my head into his bare shoulder. "I never dreamed that something like that could happen," I said.

"Thank God it did." He kissed my hair. There was humor in his voice as he added, "It almost killed me to hold out that long, but it was more than worth it in the end. That was amazing, Laura."

I yawned.

"I'm glad you feel the same way." His amusement was more perceptible now.

"I'm sleepy."

"Then go to sleep, my love. We have six lovely days ahead of us with no responsibilities. You'll need your rest for what I have in mind."

I yawned again and slid down into the bed, trying to rearrange my very disordered night dress. "Are you coming?"

"I am."

He slid down next to me and took me in his arms. "I wish we could spend the rest of our lives like this," I mumbled.

I thought I heard him say, "So do I," before sleep overtook me.

*

Our week in Hythe was wonderful. During the day we toured the area. We looked at some medieval buildings and a Saxon/Norman church. Hythe is one of the Cinque Ports along with Hastings, New Romney, Dover and Sandwich. The ports all lie at the eastern end of the Channel, where the crossing to France is narrowest. They have a noble history and they helped to keep England safe from Napoleon's navy. We visited each of the towns and one day we hired horses and rode along the Romney Marsh. The weather was miraculously beautiful. We had sun almost every day. And in the nighttime we had love.

I felt like a different person. I felt…significant. I was the woman Robert loved, and that raised me above every other woman in the world. Chiltern and its responsibilities—even the children—

receded; it was just Robert and me and the intense physical bond between us. We both lived for the moment when he would take me in his arms in our cozy bedroom and desire would crackle between us like lightning.

*

It happened on the last night of our visit. We had made love and gone to sleep as usual. I am customarily a light sleeper but this week I had slept like a child. However, on this last night of our stay I woke to feel the mattress moving under me. We had left the window uncovered so the moon could shine on us while we made love, and afterward we had been too lazy to pull the curtain. No one could see through our window; we were on the second floor and there were no other houses close by.

Robert was throwing himself around in the bed, cursing and swearing in English and Spanish. I put a hand on his bare arm—he hadn't bothered to put his nightshirt back on—and it was wet with sweat. He was shivering violently. My heart began to race. He must be having a nightmare. I put my hand on his moving shoulder, gripped it as tightly as I could, and shook him.

"Wake Up Robert!" I spoke loudly and clearly. *"You're safe! Wake up!"*

His movements seemed to slow. I shook him again and repeated my words.

He sat up abruptly and my hand slid off his shoulder.

"Robert?" My voice trembled a little. He was very strong. If he should turn on me....

"Are you awake?" I asked.

His drew his knees up and rested his forehead on them. "Oh God. It happened again. I was praying that it wouldn't...not with you."

He was shivering as if he had been out on a frozen tundra. I moved closer to him. His hair hung over his forehead and the hands that were holding his head were rigid. My heart ached for him.

"Is it the war?" I asked gently.

He nodded. His heart was pounding so hard I could see his chest moving. Finally he lifted his head and turned to me. "I'm sorry, Laura. This is why I didn't want to marry at all. But with you…I thought…I hoped…I hoped that once we were married your presence would keep them away." He shook his head back and forth. "Stupid of me," he said. Stupid. *Stupid!*"

"It's not stupid at all," I said firmly. "You have come back from years and years of living in hell. I'm not surprised you have nightmares."

His eyes were so dark they almost looked black. His face was so taut that his cheekbones and nose looked more prominent than usual. He said in an anguished voice, "I came back from hell, but *why*? I ask myself that question all the time, Laura. Why did I survive when so many others didn't?"

Because of all the years I had spent with my father I was able to answer that question. "You survived because God has a plan for you, Robert." I could feel the truth of these words resonating in my heart as I held my husband's darkened gaze. I looked back at him, desperately hoping I could convey my faith to him.

Another shiver ran through him, and I put my arms around him, trying to comfort him the way I would comfort Rosie. The sweat remaining on his chest and back was icy cold. I wanted to wrap him in a blanket, but I didn't dare leave him. I said, "Do you want to tell me about the dream?"

He shivered again. "I can't talk about it, Laura." He sounded desperate.

I held him tighter. "I'm sorry, my love. I'm so sorry you have this burden to carry."

I could feel his heart, which had quieted, begin to beat faster again. He turned his head to look at me. His eyes, the eyes I hoped he would pass along to his children, looked deeply into mine. What he saw there seemed to help. "Thank God for you, Laura." He rested his cheek on the top of my head. "Thank God for you."

I touched my lips to his bare chest. His heart began to beat faster again, and then we were kissing, holding each other as if our lives depended upon it, as if we could not get close enough to each other. He pushed me back upon the bed and loomed over me. I locked my hands behind his neck and surrendered to him, surrendered to the hot drenching pleasure that was sweeping through my body, surrendered to the need and the joy and the love that was my husband.

Chapter Twenty-One

Robert and I went to the nursery as soon as we returned. The girls were seated around the big nursery table with Nanny. They each had a book.

Nanny saw us first and stood up, pronouncing our names. It was a matter of seconds before the girls saw us too. The three of them jumped up and ran to greet us. I had to lift Rosie into my arms she was so insistent. Margaret and Elizabeth hugged me and, when Robert bent, they kissed his cheek. After the greeting we all returned to the table, the girls and I sitting on the little chairs and Robert, who could not possibly fit at that table, standing behind me. We had agreed that I should be the one to speak, and so I began by telling them I would not be sleeping in the nursery with them any longer.

Margaret and Elizabeth did not react at all. I suspect they remembered their parents sharing the same room. But Rosie burst into tears.

"Married people always share rooms," I told her gently but firmly. "Papa and I are married now so it's proper for me to sleep in his room."

"But Papa doesn't *need* you the way I do," Rosie sobbed. "He's all grown up. He can sleep by himself. You'll be on another *floor,* Mama. Suppose something happens to me in the night and you're not there!"

"Nanny will still be here, and you'll have a new governess soon. You also have Margaret and Elizabeth. You will most certainly not be alone, Rosie."

At the words "new governess," loud protests arose from all three girls. I was conflicted about this myself. Robert was insistent that I could not be a full-time governess. He said the duties that would attend my role as his wife would make it impossible to act as a governess as well. I thought I could do both, so I did what I always did when I had a dilemma, I consulted Mason.

He was horrified. "My lady, you cannot continue as the children's governess!"

"Why not, Mason? I managed my household duties and my governess duties before I married."

"You were not the countess before you married!" His face had turned red. "Pardon me, my lady. I did not mean to shout. But there are many social obligations you will have to undertake that you did not have before."

"They can't be that time consuming, Mason." I thought I was being very reasonable. "I can fit some free time into my day with the children."

"You will need to do the sort of things that Lady Baldock does at Baldock Hall, my lady. Besides needing to entertain your husband's colleagues from Parliament, and some of the local gentry, there is this house to run. Your responsibilities will include the ordering and recording of all household expenses—I will get you the previous countess' account books—the hiring and training of all the staff, as well as entertaining. You should keep up your friendly relationship with your tenants—it was wise of you to get to know them, my lady. If his lordship takes his seat in the House of Lords you will need to be a presence in London society. You will not have time to teach your daughters the accomplishments they need to learn in order for them to enter into society, my lady. You will need to hire a governess to do that."

The words "account books" did not sit well with me. Keeping the expense accounts for Chiltern would be very time consuming. And tedious. If I could get out of that, I might convince Mason I could remain as governess. I looked as pitiful as I could and said, "I kept the household books when I was at home with Papa and when I was married to Sir Thomas, but Chiltern is so much bigger, Mason! Couldn't Mrs. Lewis continue to do the accounts? She's done them for all the time I have been here." I looked hopefully into his hazel eyes.

His expression softened, "I have every confidence you will do splendidly, my lady. You have always risen to the occasion."

He had trapped me neatly with a compliment. I inhaled and said the only thing I could, "Thank you, Mason."

This conversation was taking place in the morning room. We were both standing in front of the window, which had one of my favorite views. It looked out on a small lake upon which swans sailed majestically. They might be nasty birds, but they were also elegant and beautiful. I loved to watch them. I was standing because I knew Mason would never sit in my presence and I had not wanted to be sitting while he stood during this interview.

He said, "Before I go, my lady, I might just mention that we will need to hire more servants."

He could not have shocked me more if he had said we needed to drape the house in white velvet. We had a huge number of servants already. "Why on earth would we need more servants?" I was genuinely bewildered.

"The number you have at present is adequate for the family, my lady. But when you start to entertain you will need more."

We looked at each other.

Finally I said, "Well, Mason, I am not going to worry about how I can do all of this." I smiled. "After all, I have you to advise me."

He smiled back. "Indeed, my lady, you do."

*

One person had been noticeably missing from our wedding. A week after we returned from Aunt Rose's, Mark had resigned his position as Chiltern's steward. I hadn't said anything to Robert about my conversation with Mark because I knew Robert respected him and I didn't want to influence their relationship. After all, it had been Robert's recommendation that had got Mark his position at Chiltern.

Robert didn't employ another steward after Mark's departure. Instead he took on the responsibility himself, saying it was the best way for him to learn about the estate's finances. I thought it was best to just let Mark go his own way and we would go ours.

Robert and I quickly established a routine. We made love every night (sometimes even in the daytime!) and we rode out together every morning. After he returned from our ride, Robert would disappear into Mark's old office for the day. Sometimes I saw him at luncheon; most of the time I did not.

A flow of workmen slowly began to appear at the side door closest to Robert's office. I heard this from May, who had heard it from Luke.

"They're the men who do most of the repair work about the estate, my lady," May told me. "Mr. Kingston employed them when one of the cottages needed a new roof, or a new fence, or barn or something like that. Mr. Kingston was a wonderful steward, my lady. All of the tenants say so. The farms are in excellent condition."

I had always heard the same thing. It made me feel good to think that Mark had genuinely cared about Chiltern's tenant farmers and that Robert was acquainting himself with the people who worked on the estate.

*

I was getting more and more worried about May. She was looking pale and tired, and I prayed that she was not with child. I didn't ask; if she were with child I wanted her to tell me. I didn't want to pry. More importantly, I didn't know what I was going to do about it. Getting May and Luke married—and I would see to it that he married her—wouldn't solve their problems. If they kept their positions at Chiltern, where would they live? Luke couldn't continue sleeping with the footmen and May with the maids. And how could May work with a baby to take care of?

May kept her silence and life at Chiltern went on. I went over the account books that my predecessors had kept, and I sat with Mrs. Lewis and went over her books. Walsh found a darling little pony for Rosie and she began to ride. Elizabeth got a puppy. I hired a new governess.

Her name was Jane Stevens. She was the youngest child of a gentleman who lived in the next parish and had been referred to me by one of my friends at church.

"Her mother has always planned for her to be a governess. Jane's not pretty and she doesn't have a dowry, so Anne sent her to boarding school to get a good education. Her parents aren't wealthy and paying tuition wasn't easy. Jane's sister, Sophia, is a beauty and married as soon as she was out of the schoolroom. Jane was not as fortunate. It's a good thing her mother was so foresighted."

I liked Jane immediately. She wasn't unattractive, but she wore spectacles and her mouth drooped a little at the corners. What was important to me was that she could teach mathematics, geography, history and natural sciences. She also spoke French beautifully and played the piano. She had an air of confidence about her that I liked very much; the last thing I wanted was a mousy little thing whom Elizabeth could push around. I hired her and took her up to the nursery to meet the girls.

Surprisingly, the one who had the most difficult time adjusting to the new governess was Elizabeth. Rosie missed me and so did Margaret, but the one who stopped eating and didn't sleep well was Elizabeth. But Jane and I were very patient with her and eventually Elizabeth came around.

*

At Christmas time Robert and I invited Robert's cousin James and his wife Emma, along with their children, to come to Chiltern. James was the same age as Robert and had been at Eton with him. Robert told me that, growing up, he had been closer to James than he had ever been to his older brother. In addition, Papa and Violet were coming for a few days after he had held Christmas services at his own church.

It snowed on Christmas Day, light fluffy flakes, and I was certain Papa wouldn't attempt to drive. I had been looking forward to his visit and was disappointed. Robert and I and James and Emma were sitting around the table having luncheon when Mason appeared in the doorway. "The Reverend Mr. Monk," he announced, and I squealed with delight and jumped up to greet my father.

After we had hugged and Papa had been introduced to our other guests, I asked where Violet was.

"I could not persuade her to drive in such weather," he said.

I didn't say I was sorry because I wasn't.

Papa kissed my cheek and assured me that nothing would have kept him.

Robert offered him a brandy to warm him up and he joined us for lunch.

By mid-afternoon the snow had let up and the children went out onto the lawn to play. Robert, James and Papa bundled up and went with them. Emma and I stood at the big drawing room window and watched. I would have liked to be outside with them, but Emma wasn't interested, and I couldn't leave her stranded. The boys were chasing the girls with snowballs and the girls were shrieking and laughing. Rosie was happily building a snowman with Papa. I closed my eyes and thanked God for blessing me so abundantly.

Robert and I made love that night. I always felt so cherished, so safe when he took me in his arms. He kissed me and I put my arms around his neck and stretched out along him, wanting to feel his body against mine. His kiss deepened and a familiar response began to build inside my body. He moved his mouth to my neck, my breast, then down my ribs and abdomen. My breathing sped up and the throbbing inside me intensified. When he came into me the world shattered in a burst of such intense pleasure that I thought my heart would jump out of my body it was beating so hard.

After, we lay close together. Robert's breath was still coming fast and I put my hand on his bare chest to feel the heavy strokes of his heart. He lifted my hand and held it to his mouth.

"I love you so much, Laura," he said.

His hair was mussed and falling over his forehead. His gray eyes were shielded by his long lashes. His quiet voice held a note I had not heard from him before.

There had been repetitions of the nightmare. I felt so helpless when it happened. It took him so far away from me, and there was nothing I could do to help him. I prayed every day that it would eventually go away.

"And I love you," I told him softly.

Still keeping my hand in his, he looked up at the ceiling. When he spoke it was in a voice I sensed he was controlling with difficulty. "I was so angry when I inherited Chiltern. I didn't want it. I didn't want to be responsible for it, for the land, for the people, for anything about it. The war was over and I wanted to run away and hide. I had made up my mind that MacAlister and I would go to Scotland and fish. Then Castlereagh ordered me to Vienna."

The way he said *Vienna* he might have been saying *Hades*.

"Was it really so terrible?" I kept my voice soft and gentle but inside I was rejoicing. He was finally going to share something with me.

"Yes." With his eyes on the ceiling he continued, still using that strictly controlled voice. "Vienna was like a Roman Bacchanal. Thousands and thousands of men had died in Napoleon's wars and the peace conference was nothing but a constant round of dinners, dances, drinking and women wanting to sleep with me. The discussions I was there to participate in were fruitless. The Czar was impossible—he wanted all the German territory. The whole thing made me sick to my stomach. And then Napoleon escaped and we had Waterloo."

His long dark lashes lay on his cheek, concealing his eyes. I wanted to cradle him in my arms as if he were Rosie, but my love couldn't heal the kind of wounds he carried within.

Finally he turned his head and looked at me. "England lost over twenty thousand men in that battle. I got the figure from the Horse Guards."

"Twenty thousand men," I repeated. I thought of all the mothers, wives and children who had lost a child, a husband, a father. I sent up a quick prayer: *Thank you, God, for saving Robert for me.*

He turned on his side to face me. "I hated the idea of coming back to Chiltern. And then I walked in the door and found you."

"Oh, Robert," I whispered.

"You brought me back to life, Laura. Today, as I was playing with the children in the snow, I looked up and saw you in the window watching us and I thought, 'I'm happy!' I didn't think I could ever be happy again."

I sniffed back tears. "I have something to tell you that might make you even more happy," I said.

He tilted his head. "What is that?"

"You're going to be a father."

Chapter Twenty-Two

When I looked out the window the day after Christmas, the sun was shining on the snow-covered landscape. Emma and I sat late at the breakfast table. She was an easy person to talk to and the more I knew her the more I liked her.

The children were busy in the nursery, James and Papa had gone somewhere with Robert, so Emma and I decided to go for a walk. We bundled up in coats and boots and scarves and set out from the terrace. The air was crisp and cold but there was no wind and the sun felt warm on our heads as we walked around the garden. Will, our head gardener, had seen to it that the path was cleared, and piles of snow rose on either side of us as we walked.

Emma was six years older than I, and I liked her almost immediately. She was the daughter of a viscount and so was quite familiar with the London Season and the ways of the *ton*. I was hungry for information because Robert was going to take his seat in the House of Lords when Parliament opened at the beginning of February. Our plan was to occupy Chiltern House and remain in London for the length of the Parliamentary session.

Moving the entire family to London was my idea. Robert thought it would be too much for me "in my condition," and that the children would be happier staying at home. I was feeling very well, however, and managed to convince Robert to agree to my plan. He really did not want to be away from me, and I simply refused go to London without my children. When I consulted Mason about this plan, he assured me he would come to London with us and bring along some of the staff from Chiltern. We could hire any extra help we might need in London.

I subjected poor Emma to a barrage of questions about the aristocratic society I was about to enter, and she was hugely helpful. She also made a list of all of the things in London that would appeal to the children, and when I invited her—and James—to come and stay with us at Chiltern House for as long as they liked, she promised she would come for a few weeks to help me get comfortable. Between Emma and Mason, I felt confident that I would be all right.

Emma and I enjoyed our walk in the clear cold air. When we returned to the house again we settled in the morning room and I called for tea to warm us up. After the tea came, and we were enjoying the hot drink, she said, "I have some news about your former steward, if it would interest you."

I was very interested. "Really? Tell me."

"Mr. Kingston has bought a very nice house and property in Hertfordshire. I heard about him from Lady Mary Turnbull, who is a friend of mine. Her country house is in the area."

This information didn't surprise me. Mark had told me he wanted to buy a house. I encouraged Emma with raised eyebrows and an exclamation of "How interesting!"

Emma obliged me by continuing. "He moved in two months ago and apparently he has captivated the entire neighborhood. Normally Mary would not take notice of such local news, but apparently the man looks like a Greek god and has every appearance of being a gentleman. Every unmarried girl in the neighborhood is trying to attach him."

I wasn't surprised by this either.

I poured us another cup of tea and Emma continued her gossip. "Lady Mary had no idea Mr. Kingston had been Chiltern's steward, and I did not tell her." She took a fortifying sip of tea. "What I am wondering, Laura, is how a mere estate agent had the money to purchase a place like Walmsley Manor. Lady Mary tells me it is quite a large house with a very pretty property."

I said, "His great aunt died and left him quite a lot of money." Emma's eyebrows rose. "How fortunate for him. Who was the aunt? Do you know?"

"I have no idea."

"Do you know anything about his people?"

"I know his father is a vicar, and he is the youngest of six boys." I realized with some surprise that I knew nothing else about Mark's background. He had never named the church or the town or the county in which his family lived. I also had no information about his great aunt.

Emma frowned. "That doesn't tell me much."

I thought of something else. "He was at Eton when Robert was there. That was how he got the position as steward here. Robert wrote him a recommendation."

She smiled. "Did he? Well that is reassuring news."

I frowned at her in bewilderment. "Why are you so interested in Mr. Kingston?"

She laughed. "For the usual reason, my dear Laura. My husband's cousin has a marriageable daughter on her hands. Anne is lovely and accomplished but she has no dowry. I thought perhaps she might suit Mr. Kingston. What do you think? Her bloodline is good. That might appeal to him."

I felt a surge of sympathy for this Anne, who was lovely and accomplished and needed a man if she wanted to have a decent life. She sounded as if she was exactly what Mark would be looking for, but I held my tongue.

"Have a scone," I said, and we changed the topic.

*

James and Robert had played billiards after dinner and I sat up waiting for Robert to return to our bedroom. He was surprised to see me in my robe and slippers sitting before the fire. "Laura! Are you all right?"

"I'm fine. I waited for you because I have some news about Mark I thought might interest you. I know you respected him and I thought you would be happy to learn he has found himself quite a nice situation."

He came across the thick rug and took the other chair that was placed before the fire. He stretched his long legs toward the heat and said, "I also have something to tell you about Kingston, but tell me your news first."

When I finished repeating what Emma had told me, Robert shook his head and said softly, "That cunning bastard."

I was shocked. "I thought you liked Mark! You were the one who gave him a reference so he could get the position at Chiltern!"

He frowned. Then, "I never gave him a reference. Where did you hear that?"

"I think...I think Mark told me."

"He probably forged it."

I stared at Robert in shock. "You never gave him a reference?"

"He never asked me for a reference, and I wouldn't have given him one if he did. I didn't like him when we were at Eton, and I didn't like him when I found him here at Chiltern when I returned."

By now I was beyond shock. "You didn't like Mark? Then why were you so nice to him? Why did you keep him on?"

"For two reasons—one because you liked him, Laura. He was your friend, and I loved you, and...well, I didn't want you to think badly of me."

I was having a hard time digesting this information. "Why didn't you like him, Robert? He was a very likable person."

"He manipulates people. I saw it at school. He would collect a group of boys—always younger boys—and make them adore him. He needed admiration, and he saw me as a rival. At first he tried to add me to his collection of admirers, but I resisted. Then he pretended to be bewildered by my hostility."

"But he always said such flattering things about you, Robert!"

He rubbed his eyes and said in a weary voice, "You are not going to like what I am about to tell you, Laura."

"If you are going to tell me that Mark was not the person he pretended to be, I won't be surprised."

Robert had been staring at the coals in the fireplace but at these words his head snapped around and he looked at me.

I said, "Mark was furious when he heard about our engagement. He told me he had been planning to marry me himself"

Robert scowled.

It was hard to talk about this, but I had to tell Robert. "I was a lady, he said. I would know how to run the household of an important man."

Robert's scowl deepened as I went on. "He never once said he loved me. What he valued was my usefulness. People liked me, he said. That would be helpful to him. He wants to sit in the Commons, Robert. He wants to be an important man."

"Well that is not going to happen," my husband said grimly. "You asked me the reason I kept him on? It's true that I didn't want you to think badly of me but there was another reason. Kingston has been stealing from Chiltern during his entire tenure here. There was no great aunt, Laura. He got that money out of Chiltern."

I stared at him and something stirred in my brain. "All of those workmen you have been interviewing. Have you been looking for…evidence?"

"Yes. And I found it. The reason Kingston was such a wonderful steward? He took money out of every repair he authorized around the estate. I asked the workmen what they were paid and I compared it to the amount listed in Kingston's account book. He doubled—sometimes tripled—the amount in the accounts and put the difference into his own pocket. He did the same with repairs he authorized at my other properties. He bought that nice house with stolen money, Laura, and he is not going to get away with it."

I had never seen Robert look like this. He must have looked this way when he went into battle. I shivered. "What are you going to do?" I could hear the shiver in my voice as well.

"I am going to have him charged with theft. I have been preparing the evidence so a solicitor could look at it. Kingston is going to go to prison for a very long time, Laura."

I almost asked him if he had to do this, if it would be possible to ignore Mark's crime. But scarcely had this thought flickered in my mind than I realized it would be impossible. Mark was a dangerous man. As Robert had said, he manipulated people. He had manipulated me...or he had tried to.

Robert said, "Thank God you didn't fancy yourself in love with that creature, Laura."

"I think he tried to make me love him. I wonder why I didn't?"

"You sensed something in him that warned you. He was the very definition of a whited sepulcher. You sensed the decay within."

I wasn't certain that was the case. I had genuinely liked Mark. Perhaps it was because we weren't in a financial position to marry each other? I pushed this thought away and smiled at Robert. "I was waiting for you," I said.

His face lit with the smile I loved the best, the one that made him look like a boy. He stood and came to pull me out of my chair. Then he scooped me up into his arms and carried me toward our bed. "Did I ever tell you how much I love you?" he asked.

"Once or twice, I believe."

"Perhaps I'm better at showing than telling."

"Are you going to show me now?"

He laid me on the bed and began to strip off his clothes. "Would you object?"

Our tone had been light and playful but now I said with absolute sincerity: "Never."

He finished disrobing, joined me on the bed and proceeded to show me how much he loved me.

Chapter Twenty-Three

It was time to confront May. She was looking like a wraith, but she hadn't yet approached me about her situation. We couldn't go on like this, so the day that Emma, James and their children left to return home I decided to do something. When I went upstairs to dress for dinner, a pale and thin May was waiting to help me. I told her to sit down, I wanted to talk.

She went white when I gestured her to one of the high-backed silk-covered chairs that faced the fireplace. It was the chair Robert always sat in. I took my chair, folded my hands in my lap and said conversationally, "When were you planning to tell me about the baby?"

She looked at me like a startled fawn, then she began to cry. "Oh, my lady! I have been so afraid! I wanted to tell you but Luke said to wait, that he would find a way for us. But he hasn't, my lady! I don't know what we're going to do!"

By the time she finished she was sobbing. I wanted to take her in my arms, smooth her hair and tell her everything would be all right; but that kind of vague assertion would not be helpful. I said instead, "Have you told your mother?"

She shook her head and the tears on her cheeks trembled with the motion. "She'll be so disappointed in me. She was that proud I was a lady's maid. And now...I don't know what to do, my lady! I don't know what to do!"

"Would your mother take in the baby?"

She was struggling to compose herself. "Mama still has three children at home. She couldn't afford to take on another one. And I already send her most of my salary."

I looked at her pretty face, marred now by lines of fear and worry. "What does your father do for a living?" I asked gently.

"He's a day laborer, my lady. He hurt his back two years ago and he can't lift heavy weights no more. It's hard for him to find work and when he does the pay is low. Mama takes in sewing, but the rent on the cottage is high. She doesn't want to move because we have a big cottage, but even with my help they find it hard. And now I will disgrace them." She looked down at her lap and added pathetically, "Everyone will think I'm a whore."

I said, "No one who knows you will believe that, May."

They won't because Luke is going to marry you.

I shut my lips on that thought and said out loud, "What does Luke have to say about this?"

"He never meant for this to happen, my lady." She leaned toward me in her earnestness. "It were only the one time!"

If he hadn't wanted this to happen then he should have kept his hands off you.

I left this unhelpful remark unsaid. "I want you to go to the kitchen and tell Mrs. Minton I said to feed you. You need to eat, May, or you will harm the baby." I got up, fetched a handkerchief and went back to her. She thanked me for the handkerchief and started to dry her face.

"I would never want to harm my baby, my lady." She blew her nose. "He has caused me so much trouble but it ain't his fault. It's mine."

I thought that a very generous remark. I smiled and held my hands out to her instead. "Come. I will help you, but I need to speak to his lordship first."

She took my hands and let me pull her to her feet. Her mouth was trembling and once more her eyes glistened with tears. I put my arms around her and drew her to me. She was so thin her shoulder bones were almost sticking out through her flesh. "You're too thin," I said. "Are you sick in the mornings?"

"A little." She rested against me and I rocked us back and forth, the way one does with a crying baby. "Hush now. We'll sort this out, May. But promise me you will eat!"

"I will, my lady. If you're going to help us I will do anything you want me to."

I held her away and put my hands on her shoulders. "Go down to the kitchen and tell Mrs. Minton I said to give you a good breakfast."

She stepped back from me and offered a trembly smile. "Thank you, my lady. Thank you for helping us."

"I will speak to the earl and let you know what he thinks."

She bit her lip. "Does the earl have to know?"

"If I am to help you he will have to know."

She sniffed, nodded and straightened her back. I watched her walk to the door and thought there was something gallant about her small figure.

After the door had closed behind her I went to sit in Robert's fireplace chair. The warmth from May's body was still in the fabric. I looked at the coals in the fireplace, but my mind went to that place where girls in May's situation went when they were bearing a child they couldn't keep. I had helped a few of them through the ordeal and their grief had broken my heart. I vowed to arrange things so that May wouldn't know that kind of pain. My hand went to my stomach and the thought of having to give up my child brought tears to my eyes. I was angry with Luke, but I remembered how happy they had looked on that day I met them in London. I would make things right for May, I vowed.

I went downstairs and asked Mason if he knew where Robert was. He knew, of course, and directed me to the library, which is where I went next.

*

Robert was sitting at one of the library's long mahogany tables. He had a stack of papers in front of him and was reading with total concentration. I knew I was interrupting him—he was going through pending parliamentary bills—and I hoped that he would agree to what I was about to propose. I was so nervous that the muscles in my neck were hurting. What would I do if he didn't agree?

"Robert?" I inquired from the doorway. "Do you have a moment?"

He turned his head. "Of course. Come in, Laura." He put down the paper he had been reading and waited for me to take my place across from him. My hands gripped together in my lap as I sat. "I have a problem I need to discuss with you."

"I'm listening," he said.

I had rehearsed a tactful opening sentence and all I needed to do was say it. I opened my mouth and what came out was, "May is with child and I want to help her."

His black brows drew together. "May? Your maid? She's going to have a baby?"

"Yes."

"Who is the father?"

"Luke."

"Ah." He leaned back in his chair and sighed. "These things happen, Laura. I'm sure it's not the first time a maid has found herself in trouble."

I inhaled. "And what is usually done when that 'trouble' is found out?"

"I believe the maid is usually dismissed. I can remember such a thing happening when I was a boy. I heard my mother saying that Lucy—I remember her name was Lucy—would not be a good example to the rest of the female servants."

"I am not going to dismiss May." If I were a dragon, fire would be shooting out of my nostrils. "Luke is more to blame than May is! He's older and he ought to have known better. Would you dismiss him too?"

Robert looked a little startled and when he didn't answer immediately, I said, "Hah! I knew it! It's the woman who always gets the blame!"

Robert held up a hand. "Laura, I said nothing about dismissing May. I only said that would be the usual course of action. You and I are a bit more advanced than that, I think."

That sounded better. The dragon fire died down to a smolder. "I have a plan," I said.

He nodded and said, "What do you want to do?"

The tension that had been making my neck hurt began to drain away. Robert was going to help. I gave him a rather trembly smile and told him what I had decided. "The first problem is what to do with the baby. I had hoped that May's mother could take him, but her parents haven't the income to feed another mouth. May's father hurt his back two years ago and lost his job. He has been reduced to hiring himself out as a day laborer, and you know what a pittance that brings in, Robert."

"I do."

I leaned toward him and said, "I want to pay May's parents to take care of the baby. He or she will be much better off with grandparents than with some stranger. If you pay them enough to cover their rent, her father might not have to keep doing day work. I'm sure it's damaging his back even more."

Robert's gaze drifted to the top of the bookshelf that was directly behind me. He looked thoughtful and I said a prayer that he would agree with my idea.

"There is one problem with this plan of yours," he said finally.

"What problem?" I asked.

"The problem is May's father. No man likes to think himself useless, Laura. Her father might be glad of extra income, but I think he would feel better if he was contributing his share."

"But you just agreed that day laborers don't earn much money! And he shouldn't be doing work that hurts his back even more!"

"I'm sure we can find him some work on the estate that doesn't involve hard labor," he said reassuringly. "If he is earning a decent wage I don't think he'd mind you paying May's mother for taking care of the baby."

I felt as if I were glowing from within, I was so happy. "Thank you, Robert! You are the kindest man in the world."

"Nonsense." He flapped his hand as if shooing away a fly. "It's easy to be kind when you are happy. And, thanks to you, I can honestly say that I am a happy man." There was a note of wonder in his voice as he spoke those words, and I wanted to hold him in my arms and tell him how much I loved him. but his fingers were starting to inch toward the discarded papers, and I said apologetically, "There is one more thing...."

He withdrew his hand and said, with absolute courtesy, "And what is that?"

"I want May and Luke to get married. I don't want her baby to be branded as a bastard."

"Ahh." Robert leaned back in his chair and lifted his eyebrows. "That is a different kind of problem."

"I know."

"You do know that servants are not allowed to marry."

"That is an inhumane rule."

"Perhaps it is," he agreed. "It exists because wealthy families don't want servants to have any responsibilities except the duty they owe to the family. They also have no way to house married servants and their inevitable progeny."

This was not something I was willing to let go. "I want May to be respectable and her baby to be legitimate. And she and Luke are in love! I've seen them together and it's clear as glass. They love each other and they should be allowed to marry."

His voice was patient and his question was difficult to answer. "Luke became a footman because he is tall and good-looking. In general, those are the two qualifications for any young man to be a footman. Does Luke have any skills other than his looks? Any way of earning money to support a family?"

I had questioned May on this very subject and I replied reluctantly, "He is the seventh child of one of Sir Henry Brooks' tenants."

Robert looked as if he had expected an answer like that. "So they will need to keep their present positions. If they do that, they need to live in this house. May has her own room, but it is hardly big enough to accommodate Luke as well. Not to mention the other children she is certain to bear. Will her mother want to take them in as well?"

"I don't want that darling little baby to be a bastard." I was close to tears. When I was carrying Rosie I had cried for months.

Robert saw the tears in my eyes and jumped up. He came around the table, pulled me to my feet and put his arms around me. "Don't cry, Laura. Please don't cry. We'll find a way out of this. I just need some time to think."

"Of course," I sobbed into his shirt. "Do you know May's baby is going to be the same age as ours?"

"I realize that."

"It's so unfair that our baby will have everything perfect. He'll have his mother and father, a warm and cozy room, a nanny to take care of him, all the food he needs, all the love he needs...." I ran out of words.

At this point Mason came in the door. I kept my face hidden in Robert's wet shirtfront as Mason said, "I am sorry to interrupt you, my lord, but you asked to be informed when Mr. Gleason arrived."

"Thank you, Mason," Robert said calmly. "If you will put him in the blue salon I shall be along shortly."

I heard the library door close behind Mason and lifted my face from Robert's shirt. There was worry in his beautiful gray eyes. I knew it was worry for me and I felt badly that I had burdened him. But I had to find a way for May and Luke and their baby.

He kissed me lightly on the lips and told me to go take a nap. He said he wanted to speak to Luke before we made any definite plans.

I nodded, said, "Thank you, Robert," in a watery voice, and went back to my room where I did indeed take a nap.

Chapter Twenty-Four

When I awoke it was teatime in the nursery and I went upstairs to join my girls. Earlier Miss Stevens had taken the three of them to the stables so they could ride their horses in the ring, which had been cleared of snow. They all had red cheeks and bright smiles and both Margaret and Elizabeth made a point of praising Rosie for how well she was doing with her pony. Rosie's little face was wreathed in smiles.

The nursery party was hungry from spending time outdoors in the cold air. I contented myself with a cup of tea and a slice of bread. I listened to the happy chatter going on around me and said a silent *thank you* to Miss Stevens. I told myself if the children were happy, I was happy. I hugged and kissed the girls when I left and promised to take them for a walk the following day.

Being with the children had cheered me up, but once I returned to my room the worry about May returned. Robert had pointed out the obstacles that lay in the way of a marriage between servants and the picture he painted was dismal. To be honest, I had never thought much about the private lives of servants. My father had only employed a housekeeper and two women from the parish who came in a few times a week.

When I became the Countess of Chiltern the indoor servants alone numbered sixty-two. The stables and gardens probably employed fifty more. My responsibility, however, was to the indoor staff. I had to make certain they were healthy, that they had new clothing each year, that they did their jobs cheerfully. I had recently made a tour of the attic rooms they lived in and determined to replace most of the beds—some of them sagged so badly they were almost on the floor. But I had never given a thought to their social lives.

May did not live in the attic. Because she was my personal maid she had a room in the house. Would it be possible for Luke to move in with her?

I knew what Robert's answer to that question would be. Such an arrangement would upset the strict servant hierarchy that all great houses lived by. May was not the problem. Along with the housekeeper, she ranked as the highest of the female servants. Luke, however, was a footman. Mason would be very upset if suddenly a lowly footman was elevated to equality with him.

Status was as important among the servants as it was among the aristocracy. May's counterpart on the male side was MacAlister, Robert's valet. He was a tall, lanky Scot with black hair and bristling black brows. I knew him, of course, but I always found him a bit intimidating. He was not the sort of man you could make conversation with. It was clear, however, that he was devoted to Robert. And I never forgot that he was the one who had taken care of Robert when he was wounded.

Dinner time arrived and May appeared at her usual time to help me dress. She didn't say anything, but the anxiety in her eyes was evident. I told her I had spoken to Robert. "Don't worry, May. His lordship will make some arrangements for you."

I could see my vague reassurance hadn't reassured her at all, but I didn't have anything else to offer. She buttoned the back of my gown in silence and when I sat in front of the dressing table she did my hair in silence too. Her face looked pinched and her eyes were too big. As she was fastening a necklace around my neck she said in a low voice, "I ain't going to give away this baby, my lady."

"His lordship is not going to ask you to do that, May," I said.

She nodded briefly. I could see she was on the point of tears, and I hastened to assure her that we would find a solution for her and Luke and the baby.

She didn't look as if she believed me.

*

It was the first time since James and family had left that Robert and I were alone for dinner. I was desperate to talk about May, but with Mason and two footmen standing ready to assist us, we were forced to find other topics. When I rose to retire, Robert rose as well. "Let us go to the library," he said.

Mason's eyebrows rose almost to his hairline. "Shall I have tea brought to the library, your lordship?" His voice was quiet and even, but I could hear the disapproval lurking beneath. He was a man who worshipped tradition. I imagined what he would probably think about May and Luke and doubted it would be kind.

The coal in the library fireplace was burning nicely and Robert and I took the chairs closest to it. He said, "I think I might have an answer to May's problem. You will have to tell me if you agree or not."

Intense relief flooded throughout my body. "I knew you would find a way!"

"Listen to what I propose before you embrace it," he said.

I nodded three times. "I'm listening."

"MacAlister is not happy living in England," he began.

MacAlister? I clenched my teeth to stop myself from talking. I nodded.

"I own a castle in Scotland which is very near MacAlister's home. I have decided to retire the man who has been the factor there forever. He will receive a handsome allowance for the rest of his life and I heard by post yesterday that he is agreeable to the arrangement. He will be happy to stay on for a short while to show the new man how to go on."

He had been looking toward the fire and now he paused and turned his head to look at me. "I am making MacAlister the new factor. He will be going home."

"I am happy for him," I said, trying to keep my bewilderment hidden. "I know you will miss him."

"I will, but I've promised to come up next spring for the fishing."

I smiled. "That will be nice."

"I am going to make Luke my new valet."

My mouth dropped open. I could find nothing to say. *Luke? The seventh son of one of our tenants? A valet?*

"I had a long talk with Luke this afternoon. He is a nice boy. I know his father and grandfather. Their family have worked that farm for over a hundred years."

He lifted a questioning eyebrow. "How nice," I said.

"Of course, he's far too young to be a valet, but MacAlister had agreed to stay on to teach Luke his new duties. He seems bright enough and he's certainly willing."

"I should imagine so." I finally got my voice back.

He stretched out his legs so his feet would be closer to the fire. "I also had a talk with him about his duties as a husband and father. As I said, he's a nice boy and he'll do his best. That's all we can expect of him."

My mind was whirling. "But where will they live?"

"We can't have a pregnant maid walking around the house, Laura. Mason and Mrs. Lewis will be outraged. I will find a cottage on the estate for May and Luke. I have one in mind in fact, and May will have to retire to be a wife and mother."

"Oh Robert!" I felt those pesky tears starting in my eyes as I thought of what he had done. He was losing his valet, his best friend, and in return he was taking on a nineteen-year-old boy who knew nothing about being a valet. And he was doing it for me.

I pushed myself out of my chair and went to sit on his lap. "Thank you! Thank you! You are a wonderful man. You have saved May's future. And her baby will have her mother." At this point the tears started. I flung my arms around his neck and wept into his evening shirt. "I am so h-happy."

His arms came around me. "If you're happy, why are you crying?"

"I'm crying because I'm pregnant. I always cry when I'm pregnant."

"The whole time?" He sounded worried.

"No." I was stopping now, but I didn't want to leave my place on his lap. "I love you so much," I offered.

"Oh, Laura," he said. "If only you knew..."

"If only I knew what?"

"If only you knew what you have done for me."

His voice sounded a little shaky and I knew he would hate it if he became emotional. I said, "I know what I have done for you. I have saddled you with a child valet."

He chuckled and when he spoke his voice was steadier, "If I appear in strange clothes sometimes, you will warn me."

"I promise," I said, laid my cheek against his shoulder and said, "Let's just sit here for a while."

"I would like that very much," he said in return.

Chapter Twenty-Five

It was almost the end of January before the household finally settled into its normal routine. By then Robert had found a cottage for May on the estate. He had also arranged Luke's duties so that he could live in the cottage and come to the hall to work. However, when we went to London he would have to come as well.

May and Luke were thrilled with this arrangement. A valet made much more money than a footman and Robert was charging them scarcely anything for rent. May had expressed sorrow that she could no longer be my lady's maid, but she was delighted with the cottage and was already making plans for what to plant in the spring.

They were married quietly by our pastor, Reverend Austen. Robert and I were the witnesses. Mason informed the staff about the change in Luke's status and the arrangements we had made for him and May. He assured me he had been very firm with the staff about "this matter," as he called it. "I made it very clear to them, my lady, that you overlooked May and Luke's unfortunate indiscretion because you were fond of May. I assured them all that if such behavior should be repeated the sinners would not find you so kind."

Mason didn't approve of what I had done for May. He approved even less of Robert taking Luke on as a valet. I listened patiently to all of his objections—"Do you realize you're putting this boy on a level with me?"—and I ended the discussion by saying, "I am sorry you feel that way, Mason, and I understand your objections. But his lordship and I have made this decision and we will not change it."

Mason was loyal, however, no matter his own reservations, and stifled any complaints or grumblings that came from the rest of the staff.

I felt badly that Robert's brilliant solution was favorable to everyone except himself. However, when I mentioned my feelings to him, he was unconcerned.

"There will never be another MacAlister," he said. "I'd miss him no matter who became my new valet. Luke will be fine, Laura. I'll turn him into a first-rate valet in no time. I know how to handle young men like Luke."

I thought of all the young soldiers he must have trained, and I felt better.

Another concern of mine was the transportation to London of a household that included Robert, me, three children, a governess, Mason and the numerous servants he thought necessary for our comfort. I cannot say how many times I thought, *Thank God for Mason.* He knew exactly what had to be done and he saw to it that it was done properly. He is a gem and I told him that often.

*

Three days before we were leaving for London one of the younger maids was brushing my hair when Robert came into the room in his dressing gown. When Betty saw him, she jumped and dropped the hairbrush on the floor. She picked it up hurriedly and turned to me, red faced and full of apologies.

"It's fine, Betty," I said. "You've finished with my hair. You can go to your room now. I hope you have a good rest."

"Th-thank you, my lady." She began to back out of the room, her eyes studiously avoiding Robert.

After the door closed behind her Robert came over to the dressing table where I was sitting. Our eyes met in the mirror. "I don't think this girl will do, Laura," he said.

"I know. Mason keeps telling me I need a 'proper' lady's maid, one who has experience with society and knows what is appropriate and what is not. I'll engage someone in London. It will be easier to find someone there."

He lifted a lock of hair off my neck and ran his fingers through it. "Your hair always feels like silk," he said. I smiled at him in the mirror, enjoying the touch of his hand. Still regarding me in the mirror he said, "Every time I look at you I ask myself how I came to be so lucky." He bent and kissed the nape of my neck, which the hair he was holding had exposed. At the touch of his mouth desire rippled through me and my breath began to hurry. I turned to face him and he lifted me off the chair and carried me over to the bed. He laid me on the bed carefully and leaned over me, balancing his body with his arms.

In the past a man looming over me had brought only fear and disgust. Now my whole body was aching for his touch. I looked up into his eyes, darkened gray glittering through half-closed lashes. He said, "I love you, Laura. I love you so much. So much."

His voice was dark and husky. I reached my arms up to him in welcome, in gratitude, in returned desire. This fire, this intensity, this stunning explosive pleasure, this was where I belonged. This was where I wanted to be. In Robert's arms. For the rest of my life, in Robert's arms.

Chapter Twenty-Six

After our conversation about Mark at Christmas, Robert hadn't spoken of him again. My feelings about my former friend were so mixed that I found it more comfortable not to think about him. I was so busy with the coming move and with my family that I paid scarcely any attention to Robert's decision to charge Mark with embezzlement.

Mark came back into my life three days before we were to leave for London. It was a beautiful winter day, cold but sunny, the kind of day that makes me feel energetic, makes me feel I want to be outdoors. I found an excuse to go for a drive and was dressed and waiting for the curricle to be brought around when a man riding a shaggy cob pulled up in front of the entry. He saw me waiting on the steps and called "Do you be Lady Chiltern?"

I didn't recognize the man but I replied that I was indeed Lady Chiltern.

"I have a letter for you, my lady."

He dismounted and stood there, holding his horse's reins in one hand and a white envelope in the other. I walked down the path to join him. He gave me the envelope and I waited for him to ride off before I opened it. It was a note from Rev. Austen, my pastor, asking if I would meet him at 9 Wilton Road. He needed my assistance with an elderly woman. Could I bring some food with me?

The Reverend Austen had never asked me to do anything like this before and I thought the situation must be dire. I went back into the house and down the stairs to the kitchen. Mrs. Minton was happy to put together a basket of food suitable for an elderly woman who was ill, and once the basket was filled one of the footmen carried it outdoors for me. The curricle had been brought around and James placed the basket on the seat next to me. I knew where Wilton Lane was and I drove off confidently, happy that Mr. Austen had thought to send for me.

Mason had not been in favor of this charitable expedition. At first, he didn't want me to go at all. Then, when I wouldn't listen to him, he wanted me to take one of the grooms. He also insisted that I tell him exactly where I was going. Sometimes I felt he thought he was my father.

I enjoy driving the curricle. It has a leather hood that makes it warmer than an open carriage, and it goes along very smoothly. The two horses that usually pull it were matched chestnuts and today they seemed happy to be out in the cold sunshine. I sang some of my favorite hymns as I drove along, and when I arrived at the cottage I tied the horses to an old wooden fence that fronted the yard. I had asked Walsh to put a few flakes of hay into the curricle and before I went to the door I dropped one of them in front of each horse.

I lifted down the basket of food Mrs. Minton had prepared and went up the dirt path to the door. Before I knocked it occurred to me that Pastor Austen's old carriage was nowhere in sight. The only sign someone was inside was a good-looking bay also tied to the fence. He was looking with envy at my two chestnuts as they munched hay. Walsh had filled a big net to the top with hay so I put down the basket, went back to the curricle and took another one out for the bay.

I went back up the path to the front door and knocked. I was occupied with picking up the basket when the door opened. Before I could say a word, strong hands grabbed me and pulled me inside. I was so concerned with not dropping the basket that I didn't immediately look at the person I assumed was trying to help me. "I'm fine! I'm fine! Let me go!" I said sharply, trying to pull away. Then I looked up and saw Mark.

I was so stunned I was speechless.

"You did bring food," he said. He reached around me and closed the door. "You were always kind, Laura. I knew an old and hungry woman would bring you running." He took the basket from me, put it on the floor then grasped my left upper arm with iron fingers.

I found my voice. "Mark! What are you doing here?" I tried to pull away from his grip. "Are you the one who sent me that note?"

He laughed. "Of course I sent you that note. I've kidnapped you, Laura."

I stared up at him. "Kidnapped me? What do you mean?"

His beautiful blue eyes were cold as ice. "I was visited by my local squire yesterday in his capacity as magistrate. It seems your husband has charged me with embezzling a large sum of money from his estate."

"Oh." I lifted my chin and said, "You did steal money, Mark. Robert has proof."

Mark's hand tightened on my arm. Tears stung my eyes and I winced in pain. He said, "Do you know what this will mean for me, Laura? They will send me to London to be tried. They will believe Chiltern, of course, and I will be stripped of everything I have worked so hard for! I may even be hanged! I will be if Chiltern has his way. He has always hated me."

Mark felt he should be forgiven because he had worked hard to steal Robert's money. I refrained from pointing out the irony and said instead, "So you have kidnapped me to make Robert withdraw his charges against you?"

Without answering, Mark pulled me away from the door and into a tiny sitting room. The only furniture in the room was a heavy wooden chair, which stood before the empty fireplace. He began to drag me toward it when I noticed that a pile of ropes was heaped in front of the fireplace. He was going to tie me up.

I panicked and tried to kick him. He pulled one of my arms behind my back and twisted it upward.

Excruciating pain shot through my arm and shoulder. My heart was beating like a wild drum. "Don't," I managed to say. "Don't do this Mark!"

He said, "I am going to tie you to that chair and you are going to cooperate, Laura. Is that clear?"

Through the stabbing red-hot pain I stuttered, "Y...yes."

"Good." He bent, picked up the ropes, and shoved me into the chair. I sat quietly while he tied my hands and feet to the sturdy wood.

Once he finished, he came around the chair to face me. My arm and shoulder still hurt, but I clenched my teeth and glared at him. I would not give Mark the pleasure of seeing me cry.

His face was expressionless as his eyes slowly went over my body. The wool pelisse I was wearing hid any hint of my pregnancy. Finally he looked into my eyes and said, "I've wanted you from the first moment I saw you. Did you know that, Laura?"

I was icy with fear—fear for myself and for my unborn child. I said as steadily as I could, "If you touch me, Robert will kill you."

His mouth twisted. *"Robert. "Robert, Robert, Robert.... I was good enough for you until he came home!"

His eyes glittered and he leaned over me so his body blocked any view of the room. He put his face close to mine and almost hissed as he said, "Do you think I liked being Chiltern's steward? Do you think I liked being an insignificant underling to someone who was my inferior in every way except birth?"

His breath smelled of wine. I struggled to keep calm, to keep my voice calm. "What precisely do you want from Robert, Mark?"

He took a step back. "I have arranged for a note to be delivered to *the earl* at precisely seven o'clock this evening, when everyone will be missing you. I set out my terms in that letter." His mouth had twisted as he said the word *earl*.

It was about four thirty now. My mouth was so dry it was hard to speak. "If you're asking Robert to drop the charges he won't do it, Mark. You were given that position at Chiltern because you forged a recommendation from him. Robert would never have recommended you."

"Do you think I don't know that?" Mark's eyes were brilliant with fury. "He hated me when we were at school. He thought he was better than me because he was an aristocrat. He did everything he could to humiliate me."

My heart was beating so hard I thought it might jump out of my chest. "Robert is not the kind of person to humiliate anyone, Mark." To my own ears my voice sounded breathless.

"He did his best to humiliate me! I was the best athlete in the school when he enrolled, the one most highly regarded by all the other boys. I was the King of Eton, Laura! Me! The sixth son of a clergyman! Everyone looked up to me. Then Chiltern arrived and pushed me aside. He challenged all of my achievements. He stole my reputation." His voice was shaking with fury. "I tried to be friends with him, but he looked down his damn aristocratic nose at me. He was too good to be friends with a mere vicar's son!

"Yes, I wrote myself a recommendation from him! And I got the job. And his stupid brother handed everything over to me. He wasn't interested in numbers, he said. I was to pay the bills, keep the records, and make sure he had enough money when he wanted it. Christ, he almost asked me to take money from him!"

His lips twitched. "He was perfect for my purposes. And then he died in a stupid carriage accident and Chiltern became the next earl."

Once he had started, the words came pouring out of his mouth as if a dam had broken. "I expected he would dismiss me when he came home, but it wouldn't have mattered. I had all my money safely secured. When he didn't dismiss me and went off to Vienna, I decided to stay on for a bit." His eyes fixed on my mouth, and I pressed my lips together and clenched my teeth.

"I stayed for you, Laura. I knew the moment I saw you that you were the perfect wife for me." His eyes were hard and bright with lust. I pressed my back against the chair, fruitlessly trying to evade his closeness. He stared into my eyes and I knew he saw my fear. "Admit it," he said. "You would have married me if Chiltern hadn't interfered. I would have offered you and Rosie a safe home and your proper place in society, and you would have accepted."

His eyes on my mouth were terrifying me. *My baby,* I thought. *What will happen to my baby if Mark rapes me?*

"But *he* wouldn't let that happen," Mark said. "He couldn't bear for me to have anything I wanted, so he proposed to you himself. You were one more thing he took away from me!"

He took my chin in a bruising grip and lifted my face up to his. "You have such a beautiful mouth, Laura," he said huskily.

I tried to turn my head away, but those merciless fingers held me fast. Then his lips were smashing mine, his tongue was in my throat, and I felt as if I would suffocate. It seemed forever before he pulled away. He looked down at me and laughed. "I wish I could see Chiltern's face when he hears I have his wife."

*

An earsplitting crash came from the entryway area. Mark leaped away from me and pulled a pistol out of his waist band. Then Robert appeared in the doorway. Mark moved quickly to get behind me and the gun Robert held pointed directly above my head.

"*Robert!*" I called out his name, but he didn't spare a look for me. All of his attention was focused on Mark.

"I got your note earlier than your instructions called for," Robert said. His voice was quiet, but it held a note I had never heard before. It made me shiver. "I should have got rid of you before I went to Vienna. I was under the mistaken apprehension that the Congress would be over much sooner than it was."

"You wanted to dismiss me?" Mark's voice was sarcastic.

"Of course I wanted to dismiss you. I wouldn't have trusted you with my shirt let alone my family's estate."

"Then why didn't you dismiss me when you came home from Vienna?" Mark's voice still held that sarcastic note. "You had your eye on Laura. I could see it. Everyone could see it. Why would you keep a rival in the house?"

Robert smiled and I shivered again. He looked dangerous. "A rival?" he said. "You?" He shook his head slowly, his pistol never moving. "You were never a rival, Kingston."

Robert's dismissive tone must have enraged Mark because he grabbed my hair with his free hand. He pulled so hard that my head tipped back and his hand went around the front of my neck. He was hurting me but I tried not to show it to Robert. Mark said, "Do as I asked you to do in that letter and I will let her go."

"Take your hands off my wife or I will kill you."

The fact that Robert's voice sounded almost pleasant made it even more terrifying. I tried not to wince but the pain in my neck was excruciating. Robert's pistol was rock steady on Mark as he said, "I don't want to kill you, Kingston, but if I have to I will."

I stopped breathing and after a few seconds Mark took his hand away from my neck.

"That's better," Robert said. "Now about what you call your 'terms.' Do you really expect me to allow you to go free *and* to keep all of the money you stole?"

"I said I would leave the country, go to America. With that money I can start a new life in a place that doesn't have bloody aristocrats. You don't need that money, Chiltern. You have more than enough left to keep up your estate and your position."

Robert slowly shook his head. "You are a dangerous man, Kingston. I saw it at school, the way you gathered worshippers around you and made them do your will. It's a dangerous gift for a man like you."

"*A man like me?* What can you know about *a man like me*, my lord? I was born the sixth son of a vicar who had very little money. I was born with intelligence and talent and I actually did have a wealthy great aunt who sent me to Eton. Then she died and her money went to the church. *To the church!* She spent all that money to have me educated and then she deserted me! What was I to do? I had no money! I wanted to go into Parliament. I could have had a great career in the Commons, I could have been Prime Minister one day!"

Robert said evenly, "And that is the very reason I have pressed charges against you, Kingston. You are dangerous. You know how to charm people, to manipulate people. I saw it at Eton and the minute I returned home I began to gather evidence to charge you."

"I don't think you will press those charges, Chiltern." He pressed his pistol against my scalp. "I have your wife, you see. I think you will have to negotiate with me."

"I'll lower my pistol if you lower yours," Robert said.

"I don't think so." There was genuine amusement in Mark's voice. Clearly he was confident he would win this confrontation. "I plan to keep my pistol right where it is until we have made a deal."

After a long pause Robert said thoughtfully, "America? Would you really go to America?"

"To New York, I think. Boston is a little too far from Washington for my purposes."

"I suppose you want to be president someday."

"I might," Mark said. "I think I would enjoy being an American president."

For the first time in this entire encounter Robert took his eyes off Mark and looked at me. "I'm sure you want to go home, darling, don't you?" he asked.

Robert spoke in the tone of voice he used to the children. And he never called me darling. He met my eyes for one brief minute then looked back at Mark. I said, "Please, Robert, do as he asks. If he is in America he can never bother us again. I want to go home." The last word came out as almost a wail.

"Take your pistol away from my wife's head," Robert said.

"After you lower *your* pistol," Mark returned.

Robert shrugged and let his arm drop to his side.

Mark laughed and I felt the pressure of the pistol lift. He said, "Now we can talk."

Robert cocked an eyebrow at me.

I opened my mouth and screamed as loudly as I could. A shot rang out and Mark fell, his body making a loud thump as he hit the floor. Robert crossed the floor in long strides and looked down.

Then he began to untie the knots in my bonds. They were pulled tight, and he took a knife out of his riding coat and sliced through the ropes. He didn't say a word as he worked, but the bones of his face showed starkly through his too-white skin. When I was free of the bonds he lifted me out of the chair and held me in his arms.

I started to shake. He held me closer and I burrowed my face into his shoulder. After a bit I managed to ask, "Is he dead?"

"Yes," he said. "Don't look. It's not a pretty sight."

"You had to do it, Robert. He wasn't going to let me go."

"I knew I would have to kill him as soon as I read his letter. You timed your scream perfectly."

I leaned back against his arms and looked up into his face. A trace of color had come back into his cheeks. "I thought you wanted me to do something...create some kind of diversion."

"You were brilliant."

"Are you sure he's dead?"

"Yes."

I hated it that Robert had been forced to kill again. He never went out with the local hunt, although he had loved to hunt when he was a boy. He never took a gun to go out shooting. He was done with killing, he had told me. His nightmares had been getting better. And now...this.

"You were right about Mark." I reached up and smoothed a lock of hair that had fallen over his forehead. "He was a dangerous man."

"He was a man driven solely by ambition and self-love," Robert said bleakly.

I still hadn't looked at Mark.

"What do we do about the...body?"

"I'll take you home and then I'll go for the local magistrate. He will have to view the body. There will be a hearing. You may have to testify, Laura."

"I can do that."

He bent his head and kissed my hair. "You were very brave. I'm proud of you."

Warmth flooded through my chilled body at those words. "Thank you, Robert. I didn't feel brave. I just felt scared."

"Bravery is doing something you're afraid to do. You think soldiers aren't scared going into battle? I was petrified every time. It wasn't until the horn sounded and we moved forward into action that the fear went away."

"Th-thank you for telling me that." I shuddered. "I was afraid he might rape me, Robert. I was so afraid for the baby."

He pulled me tight against him. "You're safe now, Laura. You're safe with me."

Safe, I thought. I would always be safe with Robert. Safe and loved. I shut my eyes tight and once again prayed, *Thank you, God, for giving me this man.*

*

We left Mark lying on the floor. I still hadn't looked at him. Robert told me later that he had shot him in the head. We hitched Robert's and Mark's horses to the back of the curricle and Robert drove me home. Next he drove the curricle to Sir Thomas Goodwin's house. He was our local magistrate; I knew him and his wife from church. Robert said the magistrate had to view the body before it could be moved.

The first thing I did when I got to my room was to ask Betty to order a bath. When the tub was finally set before the fire in my bedroom, and filled with hot water, I got in and scrubbed until my skin was red. I washed my hair even though I had just washed it two days before. I felt compelled to scrub Mark off my entire body.

I didn't get out of the bath until the water was too cold to be comfortable. Betty toweled my hair and brought me my warm velvet robe. Then she put a dry towel around my shoulders and brushed out my damp hair. I thanked her and dismissed her for the night. Then I sat in front of the fire to finish drying my hair while I waited for Robert.

It seemed like an eternity before the bedroom door opened again and he came in. I jumped up and he crossed the rug to pull me into his arms. "Thank God," he said. His voice cracked as he repeated, "Thank God you're all right."

I slid my arms around him and held him tightly. "Thank God you came!" My voice cracked as well.

"Laura." I looked up and his mouth came down on mine. Locked together we staggered to the bed.

Epilogue

Our visit to London was slightly delayed by the inquest into Mark's death. Robert didn't want me to testify but I felt the magistrate and jury should have a witness to back up my husband's story. It was not a pleasant experience, but it gave me a sense that this ugly part of my life was now closed, and I would never have to revisit it again.

Robert's first speech to the House of Lords hit like a lightning bolt. He had read it to me before he delivered it and I was so proud of him. His main point was that the government owed a debt of honor to the veterans of the wars against Napoleon, a debt that now required payment. He spoke about the things the government ought to be doing. For example, he said hospitals should be provided for those who were permanently injured, and jobs found for those who were no longer earning military pay.

One of the biggest problems Robert faced in convincing Parliament to act on this plan was that the Tory Party, the party favored by the Regent, was in power. Regrettably, Tories had little interest in helping the lower classes. The Whigs, the party Robert had joined, usually took a broader view. Unfortunately, building hospitals for veterans was a cost even most Whigs did not think the government could afford.

Robert countered with some telling statistics. He read out to the gathered lords the expenses the Regent had recently incurred for his residences at Carlton House and Brighton. The costs for upholstery and plate and jewels and china and glass alone were enormous. It quite shocked the lords to hear the total of the amounts they had voted to the Prince. As Robert said, if Parliament agreed to spend only half of that amount on its veteran soldiers, they could build hospitals all around the country.

"It's not going to happen quickly," Robert told me when he returned home after giving the speech, "but I am not giving up. The Commons are outraged about the Regent's expenses, and even some of the Tories in the Lords want to limit the amount they would appropriate to the Prince. Only a small portion of the money withheld from the Regent would build hospitals."

By the time we returned to Chiltern Hall in April, Robert had decided to create a private hospital out of one of the manor houses that belonged to the Chiltern estate. Papa told me that I had married a very fine man. Of course, I knew that already.

*

Our son was born on July 27, 1816, and christened a week later. We named him Arthur, after the Duke of Wellington. We had asked Emma and James to stand as his godparents and so, a week after my baby was born, I was standing on the front steps with the girls while my father, Robert, James, and Emma, who was carrying a very wrapped up Arthur, got into our coach.

As soon as the horses started, Mason, who was standing just inside the doorway, said, "Come inside, my lady. It's chilly out there and your health is still delicate."

Ever since Arthur was born I had been plagued by two men clucking after me whenever I moved. Mason was even worse than Robert. In order to avoid another lecture about my "delicate state," I obliged Mason and came indoors to wait for the baptismal party to return.

I had asked Reverend Austen if my father could baptize Arthur and he had kindly stepped aside and allowed Papa to use his church. Unfortunately, with Papa came Violet. She was awaiting me in the gold salon along with Aunt Rose. Since my marriage, Violet's attitude toward me had changed. The enormous house, the multitude of servants, the fact that she was in the home of an earl and I was his countess, all of this had resulted in a subdued and respectful Violet. I tried to forgive her former treatment of me, but it was difficult.

The coach returned in less than an hour and, after a pause for me to feed the baby, we all moved into the dining room. Mrs. Minton had outdone herself with a "breakfast" in honor of the newborn heir, who had been taken upstairs by Nanny. After a satisfactory amount of the food had been consumed, Robert announced to the entire table, "Laura is going upstairs to rest."

Murmured agreement issued from every mouth. Aunt Rose said, "You are looking peaked, my love. Go along upstairs. I'm here to see to your guests."

Was I pleased by my husband's thoughtful comment? I was not. I might be tired—in fact I was exhausted—but I was certainly capable of dictating my own behavior. But Robert took my arm and led me toward the stairs. It would look ridiculous if I tried to pull away, so I went with him.

"I don't need your help to walk up these stairs," I said testily, as he almost lifted me up the first step.

He dropped my arm.

I leaned on the banister as I lifted my heavy legs from step to step. Robert had dropped back behind me. Ready to catch me if I fell, I thought sourly.

I reached the top step and put a hand on the newel to balance myself. My knees were trembling. I sighed, turned to Robert and said, "If you would give me your arm...."

"Of course." But instead of taking my arm he scooped me up in his arms and carried me down the hall to our bedroom. Once inside he set me gently into my chair and said, "I'll ring for your maid, my love. You need to rest."

He was right. I was due to feed Arthur in an hour and I was tired. More tired than I remembered being with Rosie. I wasn't a girl any longer. I looked up at my husband, the father of my son, and said ruefully. "Have I been a bit prickly lately?"

He smiled. "A little, perhaps. You'll get back to doing all the things you like to do, but you have to be patient, Laura."

I sighed.

He went over to the bellpull to ring for Marie, my new maid.

When he came back I said, "Did I ever tell you what Elizabeth said to me after Arthur was born?"

"No."

"It was so perfectly Elizabeth. I meant to tell you but I suppose I forgot."

He came over to the fireplace, sat in his usual chair and said, "Tell me now."

"She asked me how the baby that was inside me got out."

Robert's eyes widened. "Good heavens. What did you say to her?"

"I told her that I would answer her question when she was going to be married."

"What did she say to that?"

"She informed me that she was never going to get married so she would never find out the answer if I didn't tell her now. Naturally, I asked why she never wanted to marry."

I paused. Robert lifted an inquiring eyebrow.

"Elizabeth said, 'I like it here. Why would I ever want to live somewhere else?'"

We both laughed and he bent down to kiss me. These last months he had been so tender, so caring, so considerate. If he was also occasionally bossy, I knew it was because he worried about me. Now he sat on his heels so he was on my level and picked up my hand. His eyes were bright with emotion.

"This baby...Laura, you can't know how much he means to me. Not because I have an heir, although I know that is important. But—he's new life, Laura. After all that death, we have created new life. It's such a blessing...it's like..." He raised my hand to his mouth and kissed it. Still holding it in his warm grasp he said, "It's like forgiveness."

"Oh Robert." I leaned forward and put my arms around him. My heart was so full I could barely speak. I felt the touch of his lips on the top of my head, and we stayed like that for a long time.

About the Author

Joan Wolf is a *USA TODAY* bestselling author whose highly reviewed books include some forty novels set in the period of the English Regency, earning her national recognition as a master of the genre. She fell in love with the Regency period when she was a young girl and discovered the novels of Georgette Heyer. Although she has strayed from the period now and then, it has always remained her favorite.

Joan was born and brought up in New York City, but has spent most of her adult life with her husband and two children in Connecticut. She has a passion for animals and over the years has filled the house with a variety of much-loved dogs and cats. Her great love for her horses has spilled over into every book she has written. The total number of her published novels is fifty-four, and she has no plans to retire.

"Joan Wolf never fails to deliver the best."
—*Nora Roberts*

"Joan Wolf is absolutely wonderful. I've loved her work for years."
—*Iris Johansen*

"As a writer, she's an absolute treasure."
—*Linda Howard*

"Strong, compelling fiction."
—*Amanda Quick*

"Joan Wolf writes with an absolute emotional mastery that goes straight to the heart."
—*Mary Jo Putney*

"Wolf's Regency historicals are as delicious and addictive as dark, rich, Belgian chocolates."
—*Publishers Weekly*

"Joan Wolf is back in the Regency saddle—hallelujah!"
—Catherine Coulter

* * *

To sign up for Joan's newsletter, email her at
joanemwolf@gmail.com.

Printed in the USA
CPSIA information can be obtained
at www.ICGtesting.com
LVHW091056071223
765950LV00030B/405